THE SPIDER:
EMPIRE OF DOOM!

MASTER OF MEN!

THE SPIDER®

EMPIRE OF DOOM!

By Grant Stockbridge

ALTUS PRESS • 2019

PUBLISHING HISTORY

"Empire of Doom!" originally appeared in the February, 1934 (Vol. 2, No. 1) Issue of
    The Spider magazine. Copyright 2019 by Argosy Communications, Inc. All rights
    reserved.

CHAPTER 1
DEATH IN THE SNOW

THE BEARDED fur trapper, snowshoeing through the still cold of the forest night, was muffled to his ears in a Mackinaw. He mushed out into a moon-white clearing, breath steaming from his nostrils. His pace was slow beneath the heavy pack on his back, but there was an alert watchfulness about his every movement. His feet were loose in the thongs of his snowshoes as if he were prepared to shed them instantly....

From the blackness, a rifle spat. The bearded trapper jerked with the blow of the lead. He threw high his hands, pitched face down in the knee-deep snow. His feet flew up with the force of his fall, kicked clear of the shoes, flopped again. After that he did not move. In all the world nothing moved; nothing disturbed the black silence of the forest.

The snow, which had been threatening for hours, began to drift down, a few uncertain white flecks in the blackness. It thickened rapidly, made a soft hissing sound. The moon thrust a frightened face between the clouds. Its pale light glinted on metal, a rifle in the edge of the dark woods. Distantly a wolf howled.

For five minutes that was all, then came that glint of metal again, as the rifle moved. It was followed by sound—as stealthy feet whispered over the snow. A black shadow detached itself from the darker shadows of the trees and crept forward.

1

The deadly gas claimed its victims.

It was a man, a short man, with shoulders like an ape, terminating in long arms. A rifle was in the hands, half raised, ready to spit leaden death.

The man jerked to a halt. The rifle snapped to his shoulder—and the dead man in the snow moved!

He hurled sideways, rolling, and flame spat from his hand. The rifle spoke, too, and a fluff of white snow spumed into the air where a moment before the trapper had lain. The trapper jerked to his knees. His pistol barked again, lancing fire into the blackness.

The rifle seemed frozen in the gunman's hands. He stood with it pressed against his shoulder as rigidly unmoving as one of those black trunks behind him. Then stiffly he toppled, arms jerking upward. The rifle turned a slow somersault, struck muzzle down. It stood straight an instant, then settled out of sight in the snow. The rifleman lay on his face, arms thrown out in the last surrender of death.

The trapper got slowly to his feet. With his left hand he wiped the coldness of the snow from his face. Teeth gleamed amid his black beard. It was well that he had expected some such attack as this, well that he had wadded his pack with a thick pad of bullet-proof raw silk. He walked forward, automatic still ready in his fist. He moved cautiously, yet with speed. Swiftly he bent over the woodsman, rolled him, found that he was dead, a bullet between the eyes.

Then the trapper did a curious thing. He slid his hand beneath his mackinaw and pulled out a small cigarette lighter of platinum and black enamel, such as surely no trapper ever carried before. But he did not snap flame to it. A thin smile distorted his fine lips that the black beard disguised, as he detached the base of the lighter and, bending over, pressed the lighter itself to the forehead of the man he had killed.

And when he had removed that platinum toy, there remained

upon the forehead of his victim, a small seal of rich vermilion—
the ugly, hairy seal of the Spider!
RICHARD WENTWORTH—FOR the trapper was
he, though none of his society friends would have recognized
the millionaire clubman beneath the crude exterior of his
faultless disguise—smiled thinly. Would these backwoodsmen,
he wondered, recognize his calling card—that tiny red seal
which marked the Spider's crusades against the Underworld?
He was inclined to think they would. For it was known throughout the Underworlds and the police bureaus of a dozen coun-
tries as the signature of a man whose life was devoted to a
long-drawn battle against those super criminals before whom
the police themselves seemed helpless.

Here in the North Michigan woods, he was taking up that
battle again, this time against a menace that threatened not a
city, not a state, but the entire nation—perhaps every civilized
power in the world!

Wentworth bent swiftly again and went through the man's
pockets. They carried the usual paraphernalia of waterproof
match case, compass, pipe and tobacco. But they carried also a
letter. Wentworth flashed on it the beam of a small pencil light.
The envelope bore the date of Loveland, Michigan. And the
letter read:

> Enclosed is five thousand, as agreed. Good work. Go ahead
> as planned.

The letter was unsigned. Five thousand dollars to a lumber-
jack! A backwoodsman who tried, with foolish confidence, to

kill the Spider! Wentworth's smile vanished. The shaggy brows that disguised his own were drawn down heavily above gray eyes. He replaced in the man's pockets everything except the letter, ran back to his snow shoes. He toed into them and mushed on with frantic haste.

He knew from this attack that he could not be far from a certain camp which was, to any casual eye, the grouped cabins of honest lumbermen. He knew that two miles northwest of that camp would be the cabin in which Professor Henry Cather was held prisoner.

Cresting the lazy roll of a hill, he paused and peered ahead through the blackness of the night polka-dotted with snow. A small wind creaked cold tree branches, brought him a whiff of woodsmoke. Yellow windows showed warmly through thick beeches.

Wentworth retreated swiftly from the ridge, made a wide circle about the camp, tugged out his compass and struck out northeast, moving with undiminished speed. His mouth was grim. If only Professor Cather were still alive... but the man's letter, a piteous and fearful cry for help, had been long in reaching him.

Wentworth carried an indelible mental picture of the letter in Professor Cather's queer, crabbed hand. It had been written with invisible ink across an innocent-appearing order for chemicals sent to Professor Brownlee, Wentworth's intimate friend. Brownlee, puzzled to know why his friend should have ordered chemicals through him, had presented the order to Wentworth. And Wentworth's swift mind had seized on the answer. Followed

EMPIRE OF DOOM!

a series of tests, and finally the writing hidden beneath that apparently innocuous order had come through.

Professor Cather's letter—it should have been written in letters of blood—had been startling:

> I have made a discovery that will make its possessor ruler of the world! This is no exaggeration, but a cold, scientific fact. I wish I had died before I discovered it.
>
> A group of men engaged me, through one named George Scott, to do some secret work on synthetic perfumes. I thought it strange when they stipulated the work must be done in an isolated laboratory far north in the Michigan woods. But, as you know, I've long wanted to do that kind of work, and I jumped at the chance.
>
> I worked for several weeks before I found out the nature of the thing these men wanted done. Then, by torture, they forced me to do their will. I am a prisoner in a cabin about twenty miles northeast of Wacomchic, Michigan.
>
> There is a camp on the Wacomchic River which is apparently made up of lumbermen, but actually is filled with criminals of the most ruthless type. My cabin is two miles northeast of that camp.
>
> In God's name, rescue me, before I am forced to loose this horrible destroyer I have discovered upon the world. I have longed to kill myself before this should be forced upon me, but....

The letter had ended abruptly, as if the professor had been interrupted in his message of terrible portent. A discovery that would make its possessor ruler of the world... horrible destroyer.... A band of criminals of the most ruthless type!

No wonder Wentworth had raced half across the continent in a frantic effort to save Professor Cather—and to wrest his dread secret from the criminal hands which might loose his destroyer upon the world!

CHAPTER 2
THE PROFESSOR'S SECRET

WENTWORTH'S SWINGING progress through the deepening snow was made at a killing pace. Only a man of his superb endurance and iron will could have put on such a burst of speed at the end of hours of mushing through knee-deep snow.

His keen eyes, sharply gray beneath the shaggy false brows, swept the woods ahead. He should be close now to Professor Cather's cabin. Probably it was on the crest of the next hill, there where the hemlocks showed black against the sky. But there were no lights to indicate its exact position. Wentworth leaned back on the heels of his snow-shoes, skated down the hill. He hurdled a frozen stream whose black waters gurgled beneath the ice, battled through thick beeches on its brink, and made his way doggedly up a steep grade. He peered ahead anxiously, moon and snow glisten providing a ghostly light.

Just below the crest of the hill the dense growth of trees stopped abruptly. Moonlight streamed into the clearing beyond and, as Wentworth raced onward, breath streaming from his nostrils; he made out the glint of windows and a low log cabin, black against the snow.

Eager as he was to reach the building, he stopped and re-connoitered. About him nothing moved. The silence was absolute. He pushed on slowly, halted in the shadows of the trees and scrutinized the cabin, then made a swift but careful circuit of the clearing.

The new fallen snow showed no trace of human passage. The whiteness before the door was unbroken. Wentworth's thinned lips grew hard. If Cather still were here, he had not left the cabin for hours.

Wentworth slid his shoulders from the straps of his pack, toed out of his snowshoes and, a flitting shadow among shadows, crept toward the rear of the cabin. There was a lean-to there. Its slanting roof would cover firewood and supplies. Wentworth touched its rough surface, found a small opening between logs. He stooped and peered inside. All was darkness.

He drew out his pencil light and stabbed a small knifelike ray into the black interior. Stacked wood, supplies hung upon pegs, a door that swung agape into the room beyond. The light swept on, discovered in the main part of the cabin a small rusted stove, a long bench with a glittering array of test tubes and bottles.

This, then, was Professor Cather's cabin. But within it was no sound, no breath of life.

Wentworth's eyes were bitter. He switched off the light, circled rapidly to the door, pounded on it. The wind moaned about the eaves. A loose slab on the roof rattled. The hunger howl of a wolf rose from a nearby thicket. Within, all was silence.

Wentworth reached out his mittened hand and caught the latchstring. Then he paused, and a thin smile twisted his mouth. He stepped behind the protection of the thick log wall, pulled the latch and kicked the door inward, jerking his foot instantly to safety.

The door banged inward. But no gun crashed out; no leaden death charge spat from the darkness. Instead, there came a fragile tinkling as of thin glass breaking.

Wentworth ran from that door as from the gibbering specter of death itself!

THE WIND was from behind the cabin, and Wentworth's flight was a swift curve to windward.

On the side of the cabin, at a distance of fifty feet, he halted. Groping through the snow, he found a broken tree branch. He hurled it through the cabin window, crashing it inward. He circled behind the cabin to its other side and did the same. Then he returned, sat upon his pack and waited.

Call his swift flight a hunch; call it intuition. Either would be right—for these are both the swift subconscious alignment of thoughts too rapid for deliberate mental processes. Wentworth had cultivated such thought flashes. His mind was capable of incredibly quick decisions, and action flowed from them almost before the thought was conceived. Such was Wentworth's weapon against the Underworld, his split-second speed of thought, his ability to think ahead of his enemies, to foresee their plots and forestall them.

And that power had served him well once more. Professor Cather, a specialist in gaseous chemistry, had been abducted and forced to work upon some secret process. Wentworth, fearing a trap, had heard glass tinkle. These facts had instantly marshaled themselves, and he had fled *up wind*. Now he waited.

Above him the hemlocks moaned with the wind. It swept through those broken cabin windows, through the wide open entrance. As Wentworth watched, a cloud of greenish vapor poked tenuous fingers out through the door. They thickened rapidly, became heavy. They spread, denser than smoke, and writhed close to the surface of the snow. The vapor became a vast, snake-like cloud that filled the small clearing and filtered in among the trees.

Wentworth came slowly to his feet, hands clenched into fists at his side. That gas was like some monster of another, hideous world, a monster creeping out to harry and destroy. There was something horrible about the mere sight of its viscous coils.

He knew that only his swift, instantaneous flight had saved him.

It was an hour later, an hour of impatient waiting, of striding up and down in the black forest to fight the teeth of the cold, before Wentworth dared to enter the cabin. And even then he went cautiously, breathing lightly, sniffing for any vagrant traces of the gas that might lurk there. But the cabin was fresh and sharp as the wind that swept through the forest.

WENTWORTH RETURNED for his pack, stuffed cloth into the broken window panes, closed the door and built a fire in the stove. He lighted a lantern and turned it low.

The table crashed to the floor,
and the bound man screamed.

Then, in a bunk against the wall, he rigged a dummy. One window he covered entirely. In the other he left some of the glass fragments exposed. Through it, the dummy would be visible. Then Wentworth threw down a blanket against the wall, where it could not be seen from the window, and stretched out at full length.

He knew the assassin he had slain would not have worked alone. Nor would men with so horrible, so powerful and valu-

able a secret as this gas be satisfied to trust the cabin trap to remove an interloper. They would want to make sure, especially—Wentworth's mouth corners lifted wryly—especially if they found their dead comrade, with the Spider's dread seal, red as blood, upon his forehead.

Wentworth feared that the Professor, his usefulness ended, had been done away with. And the thought of that cold-blooded murder set the fires of a slow wrath burning within him. Who these criminals were, or what their purpose, the Spider did not know. But the Spider would learn.

He knew now only that the gas was poisonous and that it had vast power of expansion. But he respected Professor Cather, and if the Professor said his new discovery was so powerful that its possessor could conquer the world, there was full justification for that claim.

Wentworth could visualize the vast menace that such a gas could become in the hands of an unscrupulous organization, could guess at the horror, the death and the suffering it could cause.

His own course now lay clear before him. He could not invade the camp behind him single-handed to search for the leader. He must capture whatever member of the gang came to make sure of his death. And he must learn through him the Professor's fate and the purpose of his organization.

For a long while Wentworth lay upon the blanket, waiting. Sleep gnawed at him. The vast symphony of the murmuring wind lulled his senses. The fatigue of the day's trek through the forest weighted his eyelids. And at long last, wearily, they closed....

It was perhaps five minutes later that a new sound pierced the muted music of the wind. It was the squeaking whisper of boots upon the snow, stealthy footsteps that advanced slowly toward the cabin and its sleeping occupant.

Wentworth did not stir beneath the blanket. He lay as motionless as that dummy he had rigged upon the bunk. The footsteps halted, and a dark blur showed against the window pane, rose slowly until a man's gleaming eyes peered into the room.

FOR A full minute the man stared into the room, then, deliberately, he began to thrust inward the cloth that had been stuffed into the broken pane. It fell soundlessly to the floor and behind it, a cold wind filtered into the room. The air accomplished what the footsteps had not. It aroused Wentworth. But he did not sit up suddenly, did not move at all. He merely opened his eyes and, peering at the window, understood.

Now he moved quietly, rose to his feet. Even as he stood erect, a bare hairy hand thrust through the broken window. Between thumb and forefinger it held gingerly a small capsule, and Wentworth knew instantly what threatened. This was more of that horrible potent gas Professor Cather had invented. If those fingers opened, if that capsule broke, Wentworth was doomed! Even his speed could not get him across the room and out into the open before its swift-spreading death overtook him.

Even as Wentworth thought these things, the fingers opened;

the capsule of deadly gas began its swift descent. If it struck the floor.... Wentworth's hand shot out, he caught the capsule in midair on his palm. As he dropped it into his pocket, his other hand seized the man's wrist. A muffled curse sounded outside the window.

Wentworth yanked on the wrist, jerked the man savagely against the building wall. His free fist flashed through the broken pane, slammed full into the evil face.

Frightened oaths poured from the man, but he did not strike back. Instead he struggled frantically to escape. Wentworth struck again, and felt the man's weight sag against the arm he held. He let go and, darting to the door, raced swiftly about to the window. The man was stretched unconscious upon the snow.

It was the work of an instant to twist him over onto his face, strap his hands with a belt and drag him into the cabin. Once inside, Wentworth covered the one bare window and dumped his prisoner down upon a chair. He roped him upright and lighted the lantern.

Upon a rough table beside the unconscious man, he placed the fragile capsule of poison gas. Then he leaned forward and slapped his prisoner heavily in the face. Three times he hit before the man moaned and opened bleary eyes. Wentworth stepped back then and allowed him to regain full control of his senses. The man's eyes grew pinched with fright. They shot about the cabin, took in the dummy on the couch, the spread blanket beside the window. They shot back to Wentworth's face.

"Yes," said Wentworth softly, "that was the way I did it. I killed your friend tonight. I did that with a bullet. Now I am anxious to see what will happen if I break that little glass capsule you tried to drop into the cabin."

The man's gaze swept to the capsule. His eyes widened. He seemed unable to tear them away from that tiny vial of death. Wentworth took a step nearer, raised his clenched fist above the capsule as if to smash it.

"No," the man gasped, "No!" His voice was hoarse with fear, scarcely intelligible.

"Why not?" asked Wentworth softly.

The man's eyes were still riveted on the capsule. "It's death," he got out. "It'd kill you, too!"

Wentworth pretended scorn. "What! That little thing?"

He picked it up with apparent carelessness, held it on his palm.

"For God's sake—be careful!" his prisoner gasped.

WENTWORTH ROLLED the capsule about on his palm. His prisoner strained at his ropes, eyes starting, muscles swelling in his shoulders.

"You damn fool!" he roared. "Put the thing down. You'll kill us both!"

Wentworth put the capsule slowly back on the table.

"I could tie a rope to this table," he said, "and go outside and pull over the table. That would tell me what was in this little piece of glass." He moved across the room, and the man's eyes followed fearfully. Wentworth picked up a length of rope from his pack, and came slowly back, fingering it.

"I'll tell you what's in it," the man said hoarsely. "It's gas. That's what it is, poison gas!"

"So what?"

"It'll kill us, I tell you!"

Wentworth stooped and began tying the rope to a table leg. "Where did you get it?"

"Stop!" the man pleaded. "I told you I'd talk."

Wentworth's voice was hard. "Then talk fast. Where did you get it?"

The man's eyes watched as Wentworth deliberately continued tying the rope.

"McCarthy gave it to me."

"Who's McCarthy?"

"Straw boss at the lumber camp."

Wentworth, ever alert, narrowed his eyes, listening. By no other movement did he betray that the slight crunch of a foot step in the snow outside had caught his ear. He went on, calmly tying the rope.

"You're not talking fast enough," he said coldly, straightening as he finished his task. He walked toward the door with the free end of the rope.

"Wait!" the man demanded. "I'll talk! McCarthy got it from the guy that used to live in this cabin. A funny old duck with thick glasses. McCarthy and the guy you killed brought me over here with them and they got a lot of papers and some capsules like this from here. Then they bumped this guy—"

Wentworth whirled. His mouth was smiling, but it was not a nice smile. "So they killed him, did they?"

"Yeah, they killed him. Like I'm tell—"

The man's eyes fixed on Wentworth's face. His words choked

in his throat. He swallowed audibly. "Cripes, Mister, *they* did it, not me!"

Wentworth had not moved forward, and his expression had not changed except for his smile. "Oh, *they* did it. And I suppose you think that lets you out?"

His prisoner licked dry lips. "Listen, Mister. I'm talking, and—"

"Keep on talking," Wentworth ordered. "Well, they took this stuff and went back to camp. They planted this old duck down in the valley there. And that's all I know—except that we got orders to kill anybody that comes anywhere near here."

"Where's McCarthy now?" Wentworth asked slowly.

The man shook his head. "I don't know."

Wentworth tightened the rope and took a step backward toward the door. "Where's McCarthy?"

"Cripes, Mister, I tell you I don't know. He left the camp, and—"

Wentworth sprang to the door, yanked it open. A man blundered in, sprawling full length on the floor. Wentworth snatched out a gun.

"So you don't know where McCarthy is?" he said. "Is this McCarthy?"

IF FRIGHT had been on the prisoner's face before, there now was absolute terror. His lips turned pale and stammered with words that would not come out. His throat became corded. His face seemed to grow thinner. Finally words gurgled out: "He made me, McCarthy. *He made me tell!*"

The man on the floor rolled over slowly. He was small and had a pointed, thin face.

"Get up, McCarthy," Wentworth ordered.

McCarthy got up with a rush. He grabbed the rope that Wentworth held and attempted to yank him off balance. The table crashed to the floor, and the bound man screamed. It was a scream of utter terror. McCarthy whirled toward him, startled.

The thick oily gas already was coiling up from the smashed capsule on the floor!

Wentworth plunged outward into the night, raced off at an angle across the wind. Behind him another scream began. A mingled scream of two men in terrible fear. But even as that two-voiced scream began, it ended—ended in a choking gasp that had lost all semblance of human voice.

Wentworth, shivering as he paced back and forth to keep himself warm, cursed bitterly under his breath. Two men who might have helped him had committed unintentional suicide. Of the criminal organization—whatever its nature—three now were dead, the killer with the rifle, the man with the capsule, and McCarthy. But Wentworth knew the plot would not stop there. That letter from Michigan sending funds, the letter he had found on the first man he had killed, proved that.

The Professor was avenged. Three of the criminals had paid the penalty. But the Spider's work was just begun. Behind these men, like a cloud of the greenish hell vapor that killed so horribly, loomed the figure of some criminal master.

Wentworth stood on belligerently straddled legs, fists clenched at his sides, narrow, determined eyes fastened on the silent cabin.

Here was a menace that might wipe out the entire nation, that might give world domination to a genius of crime! And only the Spider knew; only the Spider, working in the dark, could battle this fearful threat.

Wentworth shook his clenched fist at the stars. The Spider would battle. Let the Underworld beware!

CHAPTER 3
THE FLESH EATER

I T WAS an hour before Wentworth dared enter the cabin, an hour of fighting cold, an hour of futile groping for the reasons behind this ugly business of the green death gas. Finally striding back to the cabin, he stared down at the two men who had died in their own trap.

Their bodies were contorted as if deformed in some torture racks. The agony of that gas, Wentworth realized, must be unbelievable! Their faces were twisted, too, pulled out of all human resemblance by those few seconds of awful pain that they had endured. But the thing that stiffened Wentworth with horror, that sent a cold ripple of apprehension creeping slowly down his spine was the color of those faces. The gas had eaten huge areas of the flesh completely away, and what remained was a sickly greenish hue!

Narrow-eyed, with an inward shrinking that was strange to him, Wentworth bent and affixed his Spider's seal upon the brow of each. The ugly, hairy legged spot of red stood out vividly on the greenish flesh.

Then, working methodically, he made a careful search of the two men. Their clothing, eaten by gas, ripped in his hands, revealing the skin below, green and splotched, with wide areas of red where the gas had eaten of human flesh! His search yielded nothing. These men had been more careful.

Wentworth wasted no more time upon the cabin. His swift search of the Professor's equipment had revealed no clue to the gas. Even the chemical tubes and laboratory equipment had been smashed by the men who had murdered him.

Wentworth packed methodically, drew on coat and mittens and, with rifle ready in the crotch of his arm, automatic in his pocket, swung out into the night.

The wind had died now, and the cold was still and penetrating. No wolf howled in the distance. It was as if the bony hand of death lay heavily over the entire north woods. Wentworth's snow shoes seemed dangerously noisy, crunching across the drifts.

He wove his swift way down the hill, across the frozen stream, with its muffled gurgle, back over the hills toward the lumber camp. It was after midnight, and cresting the last rise, he found the lumber camp in darkness, save for one window in a central cabin, where a narrow line of yellow lamp light squeezed out.

The trail was hard packed, and Wentworth slid off the snow shoes, hung them on the pack upon his back, and took a firmer hold upon his rifle. He strode on, silently now in mocassined boots, keeping carefully to the shadows. The camp seemed asleep. Yet twice tonight death had struck at him from no more dangerous appearing settings. He moved with alert watchfulness.

He rounded the cabin from which light gleamed and peered cautiously through a chink at its back.

A man crouched over a rough table, his head, with red hair that bristled like wire, bent low. His face, distorted by a scar that had twisted the mouth, frowned in concentration.

A sheaf of papers quivered, in the grip of one corded, heavy hand. He picked up a cigar stub from the table edge, puffed twice, blowing out a boiling cloud of blue smoke. He flung it from him, sprang up, a man well over six feet, wide in the shoulders and thick of chest. He threw the papers down upon the table, paced three turns back and forth across the floor, quick striding, light of foot for a man of his size. He returned to the table, stood staring down, sat again and picked up the papers.

A smile wrenched Wentworth's lips. This looked promising. He circled the building, found the door latched. He took off his pack for an instant and adjusted a small, queerly shaped pistol within it, then thrust it back into the pack. He slung his rifle over his shoulder, dropped his right hand into his coat pocket, and knocked.

WITHIN, ALL sound, all movement, ceased. There was silence for two full minutes. Then heavy feet moved lightly to the door. There was a fumbling, and it was wrenched wide. Yellow lamp light streamed into Wentworth's face. For an instant, staring, the man's eyes widened, then they narrowed slightly.

"What do you want?" he demanded.

Wentworth's face was bland; his smile was pleasant. "A place to sleep," he said. He moved confidently forward. The man continued to stare with unwavering, bright eyes, blocking his path. Then he stepped aside and flung a hand in a welcoming gesture.

"Sure, sure. Come in," he boomed.

Wentworth strolled casually past him, unshouldering his pack and letting it slide to the floor. Hard metal jabbed into the small of his back.

"Lift them," the man bit out.

Wentworth raised his hands slowly.

"Two steps ahead and turn."

Wentworth did that, too, putting bewilderment on his face, wrinkling the shaggy brows that hid his own, compressing his bearded lips. That metal jabbing his back had been a pistol. It was leveled at him now.

"What the hell is this?" he demanded. "A guy asks for a place to sleep, and you pull a shooting iron on him."

A smile twisted his captor's scar-ugly mouth, showed his teeth snarlingly. "It was kind of you to give yourself up," he said. "I sent two men after you. Did you kill them, too?"

Wentworth's frown increased.

"What the hell you talking about?"

"Just this." The big man's voice grew soft. "You came by the camp this afternoon late and killed a guard thrown out to protect our property. Now, I suppose, you have killed the two men I sent after you, Mr. Spider!"

Wentworth shook his head slowly.

"I don't know what you're driving at," he said. "I just mushed in from Wacomchic."

The big man laughed. "Think you can fool George Scott, do you? Well...."

Wentworth, listening to the man, felt the white thin scar on his right temple throb with anger. George Scott was the man the Professor's letter had named as hiring him for the criminal's horror work, and this was George Scott. Wentworth forced his eyes to remain puzzled, despite the white anger, that glowed behind them. The man was still talking.

"You are a fool, Spider," he said. "I read about you and your big doings in the city. And I thought you were kinda smart. But any guy that goes around killing in the north woods and signs his name to what he does, is headed straight for the end of a rope." Scott smiled again. "We run our own law up here. I think the boys will be glad to get their hands on the man who killed their campmates."

Lynch law, that was what this George Scott threatened, and Wentworth did not doubt the man could fulfill his threat. Even if the entire camp was not in with him on the murder of the Professor, there could be no doubt the men would hang him if Scott accused him of the death of their comrades.

WENTWORTH ALLOWED his face to show fear. He stammered. "I don't know what you mean by this Spider stuff. I'm just a trapper, mushing north like I said. My name is Joe Koch."

"Yeah? Well, Joe Koch, or Spider, you hang in the morning."

Wentworth shook his head frantically. "No, no!" he babbled. He took a half pace forward.

Scott thrust forward the gun. "Get back there," he ordered.

Wentworth retreated, waving his hands in erratic gestures. "But, listen, I tell you—"

Crack!

A gun exploded behind Scott. Wentworth's pack leaped on the floor, and the big man whirled, snapping a shot blindly at the sound. Instantly Wentworth was upon his back. His knees dug into Scott's loins. His left arm crooked about his throat. The man whirled, tearing at that strangling arm. He flung up the gun, pointing it backward over his shoulder. Wentworth seized the wrist with his free hand. Scott staggered, twisting his head, lungs pumping for breath. Wentworth strained his arm tighter about the man's throat.

Muffled by thick walls, he could hear men shouting, calling back and forth from other cabins. Scott flung himself backward, trying to crush Wentworth against the floor. They crashed down heavily, but Wentworth's hold did not weaken. It was Scott's last effort. The fight left him, and he went limp in Wentworth's grip.

Wentworth sprang to the table, jerked open a drawer, snatched the papers that cluttered it and thrust them into his pocket. He crossed back to Scott, doused him with water from a bucket on a bench. The shouts of the men were nearer now. And heavy feet were pounding on the beaten snow.

Scott moaned, tossed his arms. Wentworth took his gun and leveled it at him, stepped back three paces. Scott came to with a rush, sprang to his feet and stood glowering, eyes bloodshot with rage.

"Clever, eh?" he said hoarsely, hand massaging his throat. "It won't get you anywhere. Mr. Spider. You can't get away."

Wentworth smiled. "I thought you might prove stubborn and planted a blank pistol in my pack, with a time device to discharge it. I did that just before I came in. You may have noticed I got rid of the pack quickly."

A man's fist pounded on the door.

"That's the hangman!" said Scott. "We'll hold that little necktie party right now instead of waiting till morning."

Wentworth shook his head slowly, still smiling.

"I'm afraid not, Scott. You're going to tell these men your gun went off accidentally while you were cleaning it. And then you and I are going to take a little walk. And if anyone follows, you won't return!"

Scott stared into Wentworth's calm face, and his own stiffened slowly. His cheeks blanched.

The fist pounded at the door again. "You all right, Scott?" a voice shouted.

Wentworth raised his pistol, aimed it between Scott's eyes. The smile on his mouth became cold; his eyes burned.

"I'd just as soon kill you now," he said softly. "I think my gun can persuade the man at the door."

"Why, you—"

Scott's voice began with a threat, but died in his throat. Scott's blue eyes widened slowly. He became even paler. He retreated a step.

"You'd do it," he said, hoarsely. "You'd shoot me, even if I didn't have a gun."

WENTWORTH'S SMILE was like a knife. "Was Professor Cather armed when your men killed him?"

"Hey, Scott," the man outside shouted again. "Are you all right? If you don't answer pretty quick, I'm goin' to bust in the door."

"What would you say," Wentworth asked Scott, gently. "Are you all right?" As he spoke, he raised the gun a fraction of an inch, so that it pointed at Scott's forehead. Scott opened his mouth, tried twice to speak before he got out words.

"Sure, sure, I'm all right," he called hoarsely. "I was just cleaning my gun and it went off. Get the hell back to bed."

The men grumbled for a moment longer outside, voices rumbling in the night. "We want to see you, Scott," one called. "Come on, open up the door a minute."

Wentworth nodded slowly and put the gun in his coat pocket, its muzzle still pointed toward Scott. "I can shoot this way, too," he said.

Scott nodded, fright still in his face. For death had stared at him from the eyes of this bearded man who smiled so coldly behind the black muzzle of a gun.

Scott moved jerkily to the door, jerked it open and stood spraddle legged, with fists clenched. "I said, get the hell to bed," he told the men grouped there. They stared past him, looking at Wentworth curiously.

Then, without warning, a rifle blazed from the blackness. Within the cabin a pistol cracked, and the lantern smashed.

Wentworth raised up slowly. He had not been hit. He had seen the glint of the rifle barrel an instant before the shot and flung himself to the floor. No one was visible in the doorway now. Scott had fled at the first distraction, and the other men had gone into hiding. But Wentworth knew that the instant he showed in the doorway, a half dozen rifles would pour hot lead into his body. Well, he had a remedy for that.

His hand slid beneath his arm to the kit the Spider always carried, a compact collection of chromium steel tools and various little devices he had found useful in his battle against the Underworld. He slipped from it now two small vials whose liquids were safe to carry, but which, mixed together, made a powerful explosive—one of the little devices that Professor Brownlee had contrived for him.

Wentworth took out Scott's revolver, plugged an end of the barrel with a cigarette and poured in the liquids. Then he thrust in a bit of fuse and lighting it hurled the gun at another nearby cabin. Snatching his rifle, he sprang instantly upon a bunk and punched aside some roof slabs.

The spluttering fuse made a spiral of sparks as it flew through the air. Behind Wentworth there were hoarse cries, the shadows of men fleeing. He climbed the wall and straddled its top, as a terrific blast ripped the night.

White and red fire blossomed in the blackness. Trees and frozen earth stood out vividly, revealed as if by the blue-white glare of lightning. Darkness dropped its curtain again, as Wentworth flung to the earth and fled into the shadows of the forest. **YET HE** did not run far. He circled back, looking for Scott.

But nowhere, among the figures that ran about the camp, like ants beneath an overturned stone, could he spot the tall hunch-shouldered figure of their leader. The very aimlessness with which they dashed about indicated that their leader was not among them.

At last Wentworth struck off into the forest, seeking him on the trail to Wacomchic. As he mushed swiftly onward, leaving behind the turmoil of a disrupted camp, he heard a motor roar out.

It was at least half a mile away, but the clear sharp air brought the machine gun chatter of its mighty cylinders to him clearly. Wentworth knew it at once for what is was—an airplane engine being warmed to life! He broke into a plunging run. It was toiling, heavy work. He had left pack and snowshoes behind, and the snow was deep. He had small hope of reaching the plane in time, but there was a chance. The woods were as black as if soot clogged the air. Underbrush caught at his feet. Drooping hemlock branches sliced his face.

Still Wentworth raced on. The sound of his swift passage drowned out for the moment the song of the motor. Then that roar deepened, made itself heard even above the crashing of underbrush. And Wentworth, cresting a hill, made out the dark blur of the plane sliding swiftly over the smooth surface of a frozen lake.

He snatched his rifle from his shoulder, dropped to a knee in the snow and lined the sights on the plane, already lifting from the ice.

But he did not fire. Instead, he slowly lowered the rifle,

straightened and slung it over his shoulder. His almost uncanny accuracy, bred of years of practice and steady nerves, might easily halt Scott in his escape. But—the Spider smiled—there were other uses for Scott. In the end, he would die. But meantime, that heavy, redheaded figure would be hard to conceal. And Wentworth knew where to search for it. He would need some such lead when he reached Loveland, Michigan, whence the letter had come.

Wentworth turned his back on the camp in the woods and mushed steadily southward, toward Wacomchic—and his battle with the fearful specter of the green death gas.

CHAPTER 4
THE GREEN HAND

WENTWORTH, FLYING to Loveland, looked up as the hum of the cabin plane's motors lifted two full notes. The speed diminished, the altimeter needle swung slowly downward, one thousand—nine hundred—eight. He peered out the window. High office buildings and broad thoroughfares lay on the near horizon—Loveland. Beneath the plane were the crossed runways of an airport.

Wentworth turned back to the papers in his lap, those he had seized from Scott. They were not, as he had hoped, the formula for the professor's gas. They were covered with figures, apparently estimates of fabulous wealth. In themselves they were meaningless, but taken with his knowledge that the gas had fallen into criminal hands, they were staggering. It was

31

clear this was the loot the criminals hoped to obtain. And it totaled billions!

How many hundreds were to die, writhing with the agony of the flesh-eating gas, so that the gang might grasp this wealth? Wentworth's eyes were frigid pools of gray ice. Below him lay the city from which the letter he had found on his first victim had come. Somewhere within that city of half a million people lay his only clue—the hulking, red-headed figure, the man called Scott.

The plane circled in a steep bank. The motors boomed an instant, and the ship slid into a smooth landing, whirled and jockeyed up to the administration building. Wentworth left hurriedly, signaled a cab.

"Police headquarters," he ordered.

At the end of half an hour, Wentworth was ushered into the square, bright office of Police Commissioner Harry Battleson, a short, dynamic figure behind a shining desk that seemed yards wide. Wentworth leaned across it to grasp his hand.

"You got my telegram?" he said.

Commissioner Battleson nodded a head, heavy out of all proportion to his size, his blond hair glistening.

"Yes," he said, "but no one answering the description of this George Scott landed here, either before or after we got your wire," Battleson gestured with a fat, short-fingered hand. "Sit down, and tell me what it's all about."

Wentworth drew up a chair, offering Battleson a cigarette. The man jerked his head in the negative, fished out a black, fat cigar.

Wentworth's eyes, watching, were casual, but they summed the man up swiftly. He told him briefly of the disappearance of Professor Cather and of his poison, told him of the letter from Loveland and the need to find George Scott.

"Sooner or later," he concluded, "Scott will show here. If we could get hold of him—"

The cigar barrel-rolled across Battleson's lips, "If he shows, he'll be picked up."

Wentworth nodded and stood. "The Grandleigh is your best hotel, isn't it?"

"Going to be there, eh?" Battleson asked. He got to his feet and strode jerkily around the desk. His heels made a lot of noise. Wentworth saw that they were an inch high.

"I'm Sure, Chief," he said, "that with you on the job, I'll get action."

Battleson beamed. "That you will, Mr. Wentworth," he said. The phone buzzer called him to his shining, speckless desk. He picked up the receiver with a frown and made his voice gruff and deep.

"Yeah?" He listened and his face creased in a smile; his head nodded. "Yes, Mr. Love, what can I do for you?... A threat, eh?... Well, we can take care of those boys. Sure, I'll be right up.... Ten minutes."

He slapped up the receiver, jerked about. "That was Jonathan Love," he announced in tones he might have used to say, "That was the President of the United States."

Wentworth raised his brows. "Love is about the wealthiest man in the country, isn't he?"

Battleson strode across to his hat, tugged it down on his brow, whirled. All his movements were exaggerated, "Not only that," he boomed out. "He's the greatest man in the country! Runs half a dozen industries. Has thousands on his payrolls. No bigger man in the country than Jonathan Love!"

Wentworth inspected the end of his cigarette. "And he's been threatened?"

Battleson threw out his hand with a sharp gesture. "He's always being threatened. It doesn't mean a thing."

Wentworth tossed the cigarette into a tray. "And yet, Love seems worried."

"I'll take care of that." Battleson frowned.

"I'm sure you will," Wentworth was deferential. "But it's just possible there is some tie-up between this business and the case I'm interested in. I wonder if you'll let me go along?"

"Impossible," Battleson barked, shaking his massive head.

Wentworth was casual "I don't know whether it makes any difference," he said, "but I am a lieutenant in the Federal Bureau of Investigation, and this sounds as if it might come under my jurisdiction also. Would you care to see my credentials?"

Battleson stared with surprise-widened eyes. "Why didn't you say so?" he demanded. "Come on. Told Mr. Love I'd be there in ten minutes. Always do what I say I will."

Wentworth veiled laughing eyes with lowered lids. "It would never do to keep the great Jonathan Love waiting," he agreed.

SO AS not to keep Jonathan Love waiting, Battleson's heavy touring car, siren screeching, ripped a hole through the city traffic, burned Love Boulevard westward at sixty-five, skidded with gravel-popping tires into a wide, tree-lined drive that wound through the kingly estate, past-uniformed guards to whom even the Chief was deferential, slid panting to a halt before the high-columned white portico of the Love mansion.

They got there in ten minutes, but they waited twenty in the rigid chairs of a stiffly formal reception room, before a murmuring secretary hush-hushed them into the presence of Love himself.

He rose at their entrance, an austere and a gaunt man with a face of gouged out furrows, and a ruff of white curly hair. His eyes were bright and he was grave and unsmiling—a thin man in gray against a background of quiet luxury.

"Thank you, Chief, for coming so promptly," he said and turned inquiring eyes upon Wentworth.

Battleson's voice boomed importantly. "This is Richard Wentworth, a lieutenant in the Secret Service," he said. "The lieutenant had dropped by to see me and I took the liberty of bringing him along, since your case might come under his jurisdiction."

Wentworth, unsmiling, shook hands. "It's the Bureau of Investigation," he said, "not the Secret Service."

Love nodded. "Won't you gentlemen be seated? What I have to say will not take long." He retired behind the expanse of a walnut desk that dwarfed even Battleson's and seated himself with dignity. He was like a king who had mounted his throne. He leaned back and pyramided thin, knotty fingers. Wentworth and Battleson sat in chairs the self-effacing secretary slid forward. Unobtrusively, the man placed a paper upon the desk before Love, then faded into the background.

"Usually," Jonathan Love began, his voice didactic, "I ignore threatening letters. I have an ample bodyguard. My home and offices are well protected by alarm systems. But today I received a threat which I do not believe I can afford to ignore. It is a threat not against myself, but against my people. My workers."

Wentworth drew a cigarette, tapped it. Before he could light it, a manicured hand held a match for him. Wentworth turned his eyes upward to the bland, expressionless face of the secretary, nodded his thanks and turned back to Love. A frown wrinkled the man's high forehead, deepened the gouged-out furrows of his thin face.

"What they threaten is this," he said and, leaning forward, looked at the paper upon his desk.

"It says:

'Unless you pay us two million dollars cash, we will destroy the entire town of Elkhorn.'"

Love looked at Wentworth beneath gray, shaggy brows. "Elkhorn is inhabited exclusively by my workmen. It is a model town, built about one of my steel factories. About five thousand men and their families." He looked back to the letter.

"We do not threaten," he read on, "to destroy the factory or the town itself; we mean your skilled workers. Their entire families. Aren't they worth more than two million to you? Have the money ready in bills not above a hundred dollars, old money, and wait for our next message. If you notify police, the town will be destroyed."

"The signature," said Love, "apparently is made with a rubber stamp. It is a green hand."

WENTWORTH REACHED out his hand for the letter. It was neatly typewritten. "Royal portable," he said. "Vogue type. There must be thousands of those in existence."

He looked at the signature, the Green Hand. The hand depicted was a savage thing with a stubby, brutal thumb that seemed intended for wild battle, for gouging out men's eyes. Thumb and fingers were slightly bent with a bitter, corded tension, as if that violent hand clutched fiercely for some victim and Wentworth, staring at that hand, feeling a chill of dread, knew that what they clutched would die, die cruelly and in agony!

Without a word, he passed the letter to Battleson. The Chief frowned, his massive face in concentration. "Nasty looking mit," he muttered.

Wentworth looked directly at Love. "Are you going to pay?" he demanded. "The usual thing is to pretend to and try to snare the kidnappers when they come to collect the money."

Love's mouth closed in a line as grim as the slot of a mail box. "I will not even pretend to pay," he said sharply. "I pay taxes. I demand that the government protect my men!"

Wentworth leaned forward; the cigarette spiraling thin blue smoke before his keen face. "Do you realize what that means, Mr. Love?"

"It means this," rapped out Love, tapping his palm flat upon his desk at each phrase. "I will not yield an inch to these criminals. The people of this country have allowed themselves to

Croswell   Tremaine Smith   Reuters

become slaves to the Underworld by precisely that thing—
yielding and compromising with crime. I—will—not—do—it!"

Wentworth smiled slightly. "I want to tell you what brought
me to Loveland," he said, and he recited the circumstances of
his search for the murderers of Professor Cather.

"This Green Hand is significant," he concluded. "I have not
the slightest doubt that the criminals who threaten to destroy
Elkhorn possess this deadly gas; I think they are fully capable
of wiping out this town as they threaten, despite all the armies
in America."

Love got slowly to his feet, leaned his weight upon his hands,
so that his shoulders hunched, so that he seemed a great gaunt
bird thrusting forward its predatory head.

"Then the United States government would better abdicate
and turn the administration over to able hands!" he thundered.
"I demand protection, and I intend to have it."

"Even if it costs the lives of all the workers in Elkhorn, eh,
Mr. Love?" Wentworth asked quietly.

Renee Love   Delaney

When Love spoke again, he emphasized each word with a palm slapping upon the desk.

"Better five thousand men die, than that we yield one inch to these criminals!"

Wentworth stood.

"A noble sentiment, nobly expressed," he said. "I hope your five thousand workers will appreciate it." He turned and strode from the room.

CHAPTER 5
A BLOW AT THE SPIDER

WENTWORTH MOVED along the richly decorated hall with determined feet. He was leaving. There was no help in this man. Whatever Wentworth did to thwart the criminals, it was obvious he must do alone.

A suave voice behind him called: "Mr. Wentworth!"

Wentworth turned slowly to face the secretary. The man

walked swiftly up to him, feet nearly noiseless, although he was a large man, tall and strong-shouldered, an unusual figure for his position. Men secretaries, as Wentworth knew them, usually were slight, smooth men whose chief function was to "yes" their employers and give meticulous body service.

This man was different. He performed the tasks suavely despite a build like a gladiator. He had a calm face and well ordered white hair—white, not with age but with blondness. His eyes were blue and direct as he addressed Wentworth.

"I hope, sir," he said, "that you will not take umbrage at Mr. Love's remarks. He is prone to that sort of thing. Actually he has a great love for his workers and would do anything in the world for them."

"Except part with money," said Wentworth.

The man smiled, moved a hand in a small, restrained gesture. "Even money," he said, "makes no special difference. It is the idea of submitting to criminals that roils Mr. Love."

"What am I expected to do about all this?" Wentworth demanded.

"I wish you would return, sir, and lend your assistance. Commissioner Battleson is a good man, but—somewhat unimaginative."

Wentworth shrugged. "I doubt that Mr. Love sent you with any message. I don't like him, I don't like his manner. I have not been assigned to the case, and I shan't concern myself with it any longer. Good day."

Wentworth pivoted on his heel and strode on. But at that moment the front door flung open and with a burst of laughter a girl ran into the hall, a girl black-haired and black-eyed, with the high color of the cold on her cheeks, flakes of snow glistening upon a dark fur coat.

Behind her came two men; one dark-faced and somber, with a brisk black mustache and a monocle screwed into his eye, strode deliberately; the other, an easily smiling, muscular youth, rather carelessly dressed in tweed, ran after the girl and caught her by the shoulders.

The girl made a move at him, red soft lips puckered defiantly, stood chatting, pulling off gloves, then spotted Wentworth and checked sharply, her face sobering. She hesitated, giggled— but she did it charmingly, naturally, as at some huge joke. Then she walked up to Wentworth and smiled into his face.

"You're Richard Wentworth," she said, challenging.

Wentworth bowed.

"I can't deny it," he laughed. "I don't care to when so charming a creature addresses me by name."

The girl's smile widened. She had a generous mouth. "But you don't ask questions," she said. "You don't ask me how I know you."

"Sorry," he said gravely. "Won't you please tell me how you happen to recognize me?"

"That's much better," she said, nodding regally. "Now I'll tell you. When I was a freshman in college, Nita van Sloan was a senior. And she had your picture. So you see, it's not so mysterious after all."

WENTWORTH LAUGHED. "It still seems immensely mysterious. Why in the world you should remember a photograph!" He was thinking rapidly, trying to remember someone in school whom his fiancée, Nita van Sloan, might have mentioned. This girl evidently had free access to the Love mansion.

The girl dropped her head in pretended coquettishness. "But, Mr. Wentworth, Nita told me of all the wonderful things you were doing. And I—I was in love with you!"

"Ah, a conquest," said Wentworth, lightly. "Isn't it about time you told me your name?"

"Prepare to be impressed," said the girl, mischievously. She flung up an arm in a stagey gesture. "I am Renee, the daughter of the great Jonathan Love!" She held out her white hand. "You may kiss our hand," she said.

Wentworth did so, admirably, straightened to catch a surprised, disquieted look in the girl's eyes. "Ooh," she said, "maybe I used the past tense too soon on that little affair of the picture."

"I sincerely trust so," said Wentworth seriously.

The good-looking young man with the wide muscular shoulders stalked in on him. "I say, hasn't this gone on quite long enough?" He was laughing. "Renee has forgotten her manners." He held out his hand. "I am Tremaine Smith, and this," he gestured towards the dark man with the monocle, "is Wilhelm Reuters, one of Love's able scientists."

Reuters clicked his heels in a bow that was as precise as his clothing and his brisk mustache.

Tremaine Smith smiled as Wentworth executed an equally formal bow.

"I can see I'm running into heavy competition," he said. "Before there were three of us, Reuters, myself and Jack Delaney. And after the democratic manner of the great of our nation, Renee has rather favored Delaney, a mere foreman...."

Madame Olga Bantsoff

Renee whirled on Smith, her eyes flashing. "What do you mean, mere? He's as good a man—"

Tremaine Smith shook his head and laughed. "You see?" he said. "Delaney is the favored one."

Renee whirled about as quickly again, turning her fur-covered back upon Smith, tossing her head, so that she spoke to him over her shoulder. The high color of her face was heightened by a rosy blush.

"I hate you," she declared vehemently.

"Hush, child," said Smith. "Your elders are talking. I was about to add that now we have a fourth rival in you, Wentworth. My seconds will call on you this evening."

Throughout the entire colloquy, the secretary had effaced himself. But now, as Wentworth bowed and moved to go, he stepped forward. Renee turned her large dark eyes upon him. "What is it, Crosswell?"

"Pardon me, Miss Renee, but Mr. Love is very anxious to have Mr. Wentworth remain."

"That is quite impossible," Wentworth said. "I have explained that already." He turned back to Renee, ignoring the secretary's interjected words. "I wonder if Mr. Delaney is by any chance in Elkhorn?"

The girl's eyes widened. "How did you know?"

Wentworth's smile was quiet. "I didn't know," he said. "It's just a piece of luck. I'll remember you to Nita, shall I?" He bowed his farewell, clicked heels at Tremaine Smith and the dark-faced Reuters and walked on, followed by the ubiquitous secretary, Crosswell.

"I am afraid," said the secretary, "that Mr. Love is going to be terribly upset about this."

Wentworth raised his brows. "How distressing," he murmured. "Would you mind having a taxi called?"

The two men eyed each other. Crosswell's blue eyes fixed on Wentworth's cold direct gaze. Finally Crosswell smiled slightly.

"I'll be pleased to call you a taxi," he said.

Wentworth smiled curiously. Crosswell whirled his strangely active body about and crossed to a phone. Fifteen minutes later, back in town, Wentworth rented a car and sped toward Elkhorn, thirty miles away.

THE PLACE was, as Love had said, a model town, squared out upon the plains of Michigan. Wentworth approached it down a broad, double-laned avenue. He spotted a sign, "Jonathan Boulevard" and smiled grimly. Everywhere were the Venus cars which Love manufactured and everywhere were small neatly made brick houses, each with its scrap of lawn and fenced-in yard. Children romped in the sun, bundled against the biting cold. Smoke hazed from the chimneys and everywhere was a pleasant hominess—peculiar to these model towns. Wentworth saw these things, and his eyes narrowed at the memory of the threat of the Green Hand, at the thought of the cruel, crawling gas that burned through flesh and bone, that tore gasping screams of agony from its victims before they died with green-hued faces. How it could desolate this entire city, lay these romping children horribly dead upon the ground!

There was white rage within him. Who was this Jonathan

45

Love that, like a god, he waved five thousand souls into hell with a dignified hand? Not that Wentworth favored the payment of the ransom, but it would do no harm to temporize.

By appearing to compromise with the crooks, they could gain time—time to locate the men who had stolen the fearful horror gas and were using it in this fiendishly callous extortion plot. If Love had any doubt that these men would do precisely as they threatened, Wentworth could disabuse him of that illusion.

Wentworth sent the car droning straight along the main boulevard toward the steel plant that now poked tall chimneys like an ordered line of soldiers above the far edge of town. It was an extensive well-ordered factory, with buildings as neat as the brick houses of the workers. A high wire fence circled it, strands of villainous barbs along its top. Here and there red-lettered signs shouted:

DANGER!
THIS FENCE CHARGED WITH 20,000 VOLTS!

Guards paced within, separated from its danger by other more moderately high fences. Wentworth smiled grimly. A formidable barrier, but it could not keep out the drifting green tentacles of death that the criminals would loose upon it. He whirled his car up to a gate. It remained closed and two men marched up arrogantly, eyes suspicious beneath visored caps.

"I want to see Jack Delaney," Wentworth told them. "He's a foreman here."

"No callers during working hours," the guard growled.

"This is business," Wentworth said sharply.

"Business about what?"

Wentworth's eyes went cold. "That is exclusively between Mr. Delaney and myself. If you have any doubts about the matter or any further curiosity, you may phone Mr. Love. He's at his home now. I've no doubt he will be glad to know you are so zealous in your duties."

The guard's sullenness dropped from him like a mask. "I'm sorry, sir. We have strict orders that the men are not to be interrupted at their work, except in emergency."

"Very admirable," said Wentworth, his tones biting. "Will you get Mr. Delaney at once? My business is urgent."

The guard jerked out a military, "Yes, sir," strode back to the guardhouse, touched levers and threw open the gate. Wentworth drove in and the man mounted the running board, directing him among the maze of buildings to a foundry on the far side of the enclosed area.

"If you'll wait just a moment, sir," he said then, "I'll get Mr. Delaney directly," and marched off.

IN A few moments a bulky, shouldery young man with good-natured blue eyes in a freckled face, a work cap set jauntily upon wiry red hair, strode up to Wentworth's car. "I'm Delaney," he said.

Wentworth climbed deliberately to the ground, offered his hand. "My name is Wentworth."

"You come from Love?" Delaney obviously was puzzled.

"Directly," said Wentworth, "but I'm not here on his business."

Delaney took that information in without a change of expression, but a slight hostility crept into his eyes. "I'm busy," he said. "If you've got in here by a trick, it will do you no good."

Wentworth looked the man over slowly. Delaney was even taller than his own five feet eleven, broad of shoulder, well built.

"Will you state your business?" Delaney snapped. "Or shall I summon the guard?"

Wentworth laughed. "I don't wonder Tremaine Smith and Reuters are worried. I think I should be too. You're a very fiery young man."

"What the hell are you driving at?" There was belligerency in Delaney's manner. His hands were still unclenched at his sides, but his shoulders rolled forward.

Wentworth sobered. "Just this," he said. "I want your coop-eration. It is necessary that you trust me for me to have that. If you doubt me at all, I wish you would call Renee Love at once and ask her about Richard Wentworth."

Delaney's puzzlement increased. "Renee," he said slowly. "How do you happen to know her?"

Wentworth jerked a hand in a sharp negative gesture. "All this is beside the point. Do you want to check up on me further or are you willing to take me at face value?"

Delaney gave him as slow and careful an inspection as Wentworth had made of him. "If I knew what you were talking about, I could decide better," he said. "But I'll take a chance. You look O.K."

Wentworth nodded. "That's fine. Now listen. There's a plot to kill every man, woman and child in Elkhorn." And Wentworth gave him the entire text of the letter, together with Jonathan

Love's attitude. "I'm calling here to protect the plant and town," he said. "I'm convinced in advance that this probably will prove futile. I want your help. Are you willing?"

Delaney's face was flushed with anger. "That sounds like Love," he said. "That's just the sort of high and mighty stuff he'd pull. Doesn't give a damn that five or six thousand people may die to satisfy his vanity. Sometimes—"

Wentworth gripped his arm sharply. "There's a detachment of guards," he spoke swiftly, "marching this way with guns ready. I have a hunch that means trouble to me. Where can I get in touch with you tonight?"

DELANEY SNAPPED out a phone number and address. Wentworth nodded his head and taking the other's arm, strolled back toward the auto.

"What's this all about?" Delaney asked. "These guards, I mean."

As if in answer, a gruff voice hailed, "Keep away from that car."

Wentworth whirled then to face the guards, apparently seeing them for the first time. They had strung out so that they formed a semi-circle, penning him against the factory wall.

Delaney spun angrily. "What is the meaning of this, Simmons?"

The man he addressed held a revolver in his hand. It was leveled at Wentworth. The others in the group had guns leveled too.

"This man is wanted for murder," said Simmons. "Mr. Love phoned to arrest him. Come away, sir. He's desperate and we may have to shoot." The gun pointed purposefully. "Mr. Croswell phoned. Mr. Love said not to hesitate to kill him if necessary."

Wentworth thought swiftly. A murder charge—it might be any one of a score of killings that, as the Spider, he had been forced to commit, each one wiping out some menace to society, eliminating some new threat to civilization. But only a few intimates knew Wentworth was the Spider, Nita van Sloan, his body servant, Ram Singh, Professor Brownlee…. No, it must be one of the killings he had been forced to commit in the woods, defending himself against attack. But who had traced a connection between the bearded trapper, Joe Koch, and the suave man of wealth, Wentworth? Like a flash came the answer—George Scott!

Then the red-headed man he had overcome in the woods was on the scene, and was behind this ghastly extortion plot. He was seeking to eliminate Wentworth before the crucial attack. But he must not be eliminated! Even a few days in jail now might mean the loss of thousands of lives, that deadly green horror might be released on the capitals of the world! He must escape!

Wentworth glanced swiftly about: Six men with guns penned him against the wall. If he escaped them, there was that fence which to touch meant death. He faced the guards. Simmons and the five men were closing in with drawn guns!

CHAPTER 6
A RUGGED INDIVIDUALIST

DELANEY STEPPED in front of Wentworth. "A murder charge? That's ridiculous." He cut the air with the edge of his right hand. "This man is a friend of mine."

The guards continued to advance, and the muzzles of their pistols did not waver. Delaney was angrily posed, shoulders hunched, head thrust forward pugnaciously. Wentworth touched him on the shoulder.

"Never mind, Delaney," he said "There is obviously some mistake." He turned toward the man called Simmons, inspected his alert set face. "I'll go with you, Simmons," he said, "on one condition. When we reach the guardhouse, you must phone Crosswell and let me talk to him."

Simmons' mouth was tight. "You'll come with us anyway," he said shortly.

Wentworth smiled easily. "Doubtless, Simmons, doubtless. I just didn't want you to make a mistake. It might re-act against you. Misunderstandings are possible, you know."

"Boloney! This is just a stall!" said Simmons. But there was no certainty in his voice, and the guards lost their tense readiness. They had come prepared to shoot it out with a desperate criminal and had found instead a poised gentleman. Though they still held their guns, three had lowered them. Simmons, himself, pointed his weapon less surely.

"Well, how about it?" Wentworth demanded. "Do we call Crosswell or are you going to risk your job?"

The man frowned dubiously, his entire face wrinkling. "I don't see as it would do any harm to phone Crosswell," he said. "Though he don't like being disturbed."

Wentworth nodded and walked toward Simmons, submitted to a search which found no weapon. Then, with the guards about him, he went briskly back to the entrance gate, Delaney marching indignantly at his side.

The call to Crosswell went through swiftly, and Wentworth got him to the phone without difficulty.

"Wentworth speaking," he said. "The captain of your guard at the Elkhorn plant says you phoned him to arrest me for murder. It was a little strange," Wentworth's tone grew bantering, "since I didn't remember committing any murders recently and I thought I'd like to satisfy my curiosity about the matter."

Crosswell said, "What!" in an amazed tone and Wentworth repeated slowly.

Crosswell sputtered: "That's ridiculous. I've not made a phone call to him today."

"I thought not," said Wentworth softly. "Would you mind speaking to Simmons then?"

"Certainly," Crosswell said. Wentworth turned to the grim-faced captain of the guard. He was a worried man now, his forehead ridged with anxiety. He took the telephone without a word, and said, "Yes, sir" and again, "Yes, sir," and again. He tried vainly to edge in a protest. "I know, sir, but he.... I hope, sir, that this won't be held against me... I was just... Yes, sir... Right away, sir...."

He hung up slowly and turned, removing his cap and sponging his forehead with a handkerchief. The handkerchief came away wet.

"I'm sorry about this, sir," he said to Wentworth. "But somebody I would have sworn was Crosswell phoned me, gave me his secret identification and gave me the order that I started out to execute." His face was pale. "Good God, sir, suppose you had resisted!"

"Then, Simmons," said Wentworth slowly, "You'd have been in a devilish bad spot." He turned to Delaney. "I'll see you later."

Delaney nodded, scowled at the guard, then strode away. WENTWORTH, HAVING his car brought from within, drove rapidly back to Loveland. He registered at the Grandleigh and had scarcely entered his room before Crosswell's voice was on the wire again.

"Mr. Love is very anxious…" Crosswell began.

"I'm not," Wentworth snapped. "I gave Love an opportunity to cooperate and he refused it pig-headedly. I'm making my own plans now. And Love can conform with them or not as he sees fit."

Crosswell's laughter over the phone was soft, but surprisingly genuine. "I think," he said, "that you will have little difficulty about that. He has been talking with the Governor over long distance, and the Governor made the same sort of recommendation. I might say that I urged on him myself the necessity of appearing to conform with the criminals in order to trap them."

"That will do no good now," Wentworth said bitterly. "The

criminals know I am on the case. That call today to accomplish my arrest was their work. I'm sure of that."

Crosswell's voice grew agitated. "You mean they'll know the offer to pay is a fake?"

Wentworth laughed grimly. "I doubt they expected to collect without striking a blow."

"Just a minute, sir," said Crosswell, and Wentworth heard over the wire the murmur of voices, Crosswell's and the incisive tones of Jonathan Love.

"Mr. Love requests," Crosswell said finally, "that you become a guest at his home. So that he may cooperate more fully with you in arranging this defense."

"I will come there tonight for a discussion of plans," Wentworth said shortly, "but I consider it better to keep my headquarters here."

He slapped up the receiver. Even the thought of Jonathan Love annoyed him, and he did not wish to have any dealings with him. But the man was powerful. He might help, if he would, in thwarting the criminals. Regardless of how Wentworth felt about it, he considered that he must at least try to cooperate with Love for the sake of the people of Elkhorn, for the sake of the world, threatened by that clutching, brutal Green Hand.

As always, when disturbed, Wentworth turned to his music for comfort, taking his rare violin from its case and drawing throbbing music from it. As first the music, reflecting his mood, was violent and angry. But gradually it changed, and dulcet notes trilled from it. Smiling then, he crossed to the phone again and called Nita van Sloan at her apartment high above the Hudson on Riverside Drive. Never was he long without calling or seeing her, and now he seized the first pause of this new crusade to hear her sweet voice. As always, it revived him, buoyed his spirits. He could close his eyes and see her lovely aristocratic face with its cluster brown curls about it, her blue eyes of mystery.... Finally he asked her to give a message to Ram Singh, his body servant extraordinary and hung up.

He called Delaney into conference then and went over the terrain about Elkhorn which soon was to be the battleground for titanic forces. And he took Delaney with him when he went to the Love home.

HE DID not see Renee, nor the two men, Smith and Reuters. Love was seated as before behind his huge walnut desk, the deep lines of his face accented, heavily shadowed by worry.

"I understand," he began at once, "that you consider it too late now to try to trick these people with a fake payment."

Wentworth nodded, introduced Delaney. "One of your foremen."

"I know Delaney," Love said stiffly.

There was a grim humor about Delaney's mouth as that fiery young redhead stared at the owner of the factory in which he was only a minor employee. He seemed to draw a certain humorous satisfaction from the situation, but he remained in the background, as did Crosswell.

Love's dark eyes fixed on Wentworth's face. "What do you recommend?"

"Immediate evacuation of Elkhorn. Move all the families to other towns. Close your factory, except for guards."

Love's face darkened. "But that is impossible!" he cried, his tones angry. "It means the loss of millions and would accomplish nothing. My interests are wide and scattered. These criminals have only to shift their attack to some other point. If I did that I soon should be forced to suspend all my industries."

Wentworth's mouth was shut tightly. He nodded slowly. "That is a possibility, but meantime, it would save the lives of these threatened people, and it would give us time to trace the Green Hand."

Love took a quick turn up and down the room, agitation in his long striding legs, in the rigid posture of his back. He stopped abruptly and shook a bony finger in Wentworth's face. "You're deliberately trying to humiliate me," he thundered.

Wentworth smiled gently. "I don't give a damn about you," he said. "I'm only interested in preserving the lives of your workmen and their families."

Love's sallow skin became almost apoplectic with a rush of angry blood. "Get out!" he roared.

"Oh, shut up," said Wentworth wearily. "This is what you'll have to do. Evacuate the town secretly. Throw state troops about it armed with gas masks. I've been over the terrain with Delaney here. Outposts must be thrown—"

Love had been speechless with fury. Now his voice burst out hoarsely. "Get out before I have you thrown out!"

Wentworth bowed stiffly. "Very well, but I'm warning you

that unless you behave more reasonably I will take the matter out of your hands entirely and evacuate the town myself."

Delaney beside him, he stalked toward the door. It was flung open, and Renee ran in, her dark eyes wide, her cheeks flushed. "Dad," she cried, "surely you must see that you can't do this with your people!"

"Go to your room," Love snapped.

The girl stared at him in amazement. Slowly her own small shapely body became rigid, too. A counterpart of Love's own harsh commanding gaze glared back at him. "I am not a servant," she said. "Don't speak to me like one." For a moment father and daughter stared angrily into each other's eyes.

It was Wentworth who interceded. "It is quite hopeless, Miss Love," he said. "Your father is what is known as a rugged individualist. Cooperation would be impossible for him. Do not concern yourself about this."

The girl turned toward him, anger still burning in her eyes. "But the people—" Her appealing glance flicked to Delaney also.

Wentworth smiled. "Jack and I will see that they are removed from danger." He bowed again and stalked out.

The girl ran after him, but it was Delaney to whom she appealed now. "Oh, Jack, do everything you can." Her hand on Delaney's arm, her face, with its red generous mouth upturned to his. "Father is not really mean, or as blind as that. He means well. But the mere thought of criminals infuriates him."

"So I see," said Delaney dryly. He covered the girl's white hand with his large brown one.

"Oh, Jack…" choked the girl.

Wentworth broke in. "Another time, Jack. We've got to hurry now, Renee. There's work to be done. One hell of a lot of it. I think that gang may strike at any moment, now that they know Love won't pay."

He strode out of the house with Delaney at his heels. They flung into a car and raced for Elkhorn. As they sped on Wentworth talked swiftly to Delaney. "I had hoped," he said, "to get Love's cooperation in evacuating the city. That would have made it much simpler. Now there is no choice but to do it without his assistance. That may prove difficult. It is hard to convince a man who is healthy and well within his own home that within five minutes' time he and all his family may be dead."

"Five minutes!" cried Delaney.

Wentworth's eyes glittered. "It may be five minutes. It may be five days. But if I were those criminals, I think I should strike at once."

They were silent then for minutes, while the motor roared, dragging them along smooth roads at a mile a minute pace. The cold air whined and whistled past. Wentworth's hand, numb within a glove, began to stiffen about the steering wheel. He slapped life back into it against his knee.

"There's this about it," said Delaney. "If they are sure of themselves, it would be a hell of a sight more effective if they waited until the soldiers were all there, then turned loose the gas."

Wentworth nodded. "Troops are already there," he said. "I called the Governor this afternoon."

"You called the Governor!" Delaney repeated slowly. "Good Lord, then the attack is certainly on tonight. They'll turn loose that gas…."

He leaned forward, clenched fists on his knees.

"Can't you get any more speed out of this car?" he demanded, savagely. "God help us to reach there before the massacre begins!"

CHAPTER 7
THE GREEN HAND STRIKES

THEY HAD left Loveland Boulevard now and were whirling on the Elkhorn Pike. Wentworth's foot pinned the accelerator to the floor. Lights bored a tunnel of whiteness through the black night.

"To reach there before the massacre starts, will not be sufficient," he said. "We must reach there in time for you to get the people away. That is your job. They know you and will be more apt to heed what you say.

"I am going to the troop's headquarters, try to get the major to send soldiers over the city to order the people out. I don't know whether he will do it without word from Love, but I'll try to persuade him. If I fail, you will have to get some men together and broadcast the appeal. Those people have got to leave the city!"

The white pools of the street lights of Elkhorn began to glow in the distance, then the warm yellow windows of homes. Wentworth tore on. A warning shout and whining rifle bullet reminded him of the guard about the town. He clamped on brakes then, slid to a halt with tires screaming. A soldier with ready rifle, bayonet fixed, darted to the car.

"Take me to Major Bentwood at once," Wentworth ordered.

The soldier glared suspiciously, the bayonet leveled at Wentworth's throat. "What the hell's the big idea?" he demanded, "of scooting into town at sixty miles an hour?"

"I'm in a hurry," Wentworth snapped. "Get me to Major Bentwood at once."

The sharpness of his words stiffened the soldier. He recognized authority in that voice. He shouted "Sergeant of the Guard!" Fifty feet away his cry was picked up by another sentry and relayed, voices ringing on the cold night air, until a man in a motorcycle sidecar whizzed up and skidded to a stop beside the car.

Through successive relays of officers that required endless time, Wentworth finally gained the presence of Major Bentwood. The Major was obdurate to all suggestion of evacuating the city.

"Foolish," he grunted. "We can take care of them."

Wentworth wasted no time in arguing. He put through a call to the Governor and requested orders that the town be evacuated.

Finally the wrangle was won, and patrols of soldiers started out to evacuate the city. Wentworth waited only for the order, then raced swiftly to a nearby airport, Delaney insisting on accompanying him. As Wentworth's car swerved into the field, a plane motor roared out. A black biplane two-seater was on the line, and as Wentworth drove near, a dark faced man in a turban, climbed from the rear cockpit and salaamed.

"Good work, Ram Singh," said Wentworth, "you made a fast trip." The Hindu's dark eyes glinted with pleasure. "You ordered it, *Sahib*," he replied.

Wentworth was swiftly drawing on helmet and flying jacket: He climbed into parachute harness while he talked. Ram Singh did the same. He looked strange with goggles over his turban.

"Get back to Loveland," Wentworth told Delaney. "Locate Wilhelm Reuters and let me know what he does tonight. There is something I don't like about that man."

Delaney frowned. "I think I ought to get back to Elkhorn and help them there."

"You can't do a damn thing," Wentworth told him. "They've got more soldiers than they know what to do with. The town is being evacuated. There'll be nothing to gain by your going back, and it's important that Reuters be followed. You can be of much greater service if you do that."

Delaney eyed him suspiciously, then nodded. "O.K.," he said. "I thought for a moment you were trying to give me a soft job. But I guess you really mean it."

"I do," said Wentworth, shortly. "Good luck."

He strode across the slip-stream of the propeller, bending against the blasting wind, and clambering to the cockpit. Ram Singh mounted also. Machine guns were ready to Wentworth's hand, pointed forward through the propeller.

In the after cockpit, Ram Singh had twin guns also, mounted upon a Scarf ring. Wentworth jazzed the motor, felt its warm, quick pickup, waved his hand for the chock to be yanked from beneath the wheel and shot the black ship roaring across the field. The tail lifted, he eased back on the stick and the powerful plane slipped clear, zoomed and spiraled steeply upward.

WENTWORTH'S MIND was racing as he sought altitude. It was apparent that the criminals who called themselves the Green Hand had a spy in his camp. They had known of him and his visit to the factory at Elkhorn, had connected him with the bearded trapper. So Wentworth, in all his planning, had stressed the fact that he expected an attack by land. He wished to force an attempt from the skies. And he himself, with his deadly plane, would sweep the heavens above Elkhorn.

Up and up he pushed the black ship. At ten thousand feet Loveland was clearly visible, a twinkling mass of lights on the horizon. Beneath him, the smaller area that was Elkhorn showed its regular crisscross of street lights. Wentworth circled, waiting. A single plane could carry ample store of the gas to wipe out the entire town. Its incredible power of expansion—a tiny capsule had filled the cabin with instant death, had struck down two men—would make two or three pounds of the stuff sufficient to wipe out half the town.

Auto headlights were streaming away from Elkhorn now, running away on all roads, the townspeople evacuating before the prod of soldiers' guns. At least that part of his job had been well done. If any died tonight, it would be the soldiers who were prepared to battle, and their lungs would be protected by gas masks, their bodies by chemically prepared clothing against vapor, for Wentworth had given the Governor all the information he possessed about the gas.

For an hour and a half, while the stream of autos continued to pour from the town, thinning gradually until it was apparent that the last of the citizens were leaving. Wentworth circled without sighting another ship, without finding anything suspicious either in the air above or in the panorama of earth stretched out below, black and powdered with lights.

Then came a blow on his shoulder! Ram Singh's warning! He jerked his head about, heard the chatter of the Hindu's gun and, against the night sky, saw a ship slamming down at him from above. Twin flames flickered behind the propeller. Wentworth kicked the rudder, vaulted the ship in a swift whirling Immelman. He saw the fiery streaks of tracer bullets slice past only inches away.

THE ATTACKING ship shot past below him. Wentworth whirled, dove toward its tail. The ship zipped into a power dive, roaring earthward with motor wide open.

Wentworth threw his own craft into a steeply pounding dive behind the other. Useless to fire his machine guns. Too great a distance separated him from the fiery exhausts of the other ship. Try as he would, he could not close that gap. And the other plane was racing straight toward Elkhorn!

Wentworth was positive.

It was apparent the ship wished to get close to the ground before dropping its gas bombs. Probably they were fragile receptacles that the wind would whirl and might throw astray if they fell from too great altitude.

Wentworth knew he must overtake the other ship, must stop its rain of deadly bombs. Desperately he threw his own plane into a vertical dive, motor straining at top speed. The earth rushed upward at a terrific pace. But now, at last, Wentworth was descending faster than the gas plane. Watching it closely, for the moment when he would pass it, Wentworth kept his thumbs on the trigger of his machine guns.

At long last, that moment came. He was traveling at incredible speed, his plane shaking and whining with the ripping of the wind. The ship was built to stand the wrench and stress of acrobatics in the air, but few craft ever had been called upon to stand the strain of such a vertical dive and the sudden snap out of it that Wentworth now planned.

Already they had shot past Elkhorn, were out over the dark plains beyond the city. It was safe to try the desperate stratagem Wentworth had determined upon. With rigid hand, feet steady upon the rudder, he strained back on the stick, jabbing the trigger of the machine gun. He saw the streaking course of his burning bullets speed first almost straight at the earth, then as the quivering ship answered the stick, the lead swept upward into the path of the plane ahead.

Wentworth strained harder at the stick. The roar of the motor was deafening. Vibration wracked the ship. But slowly, slowly the nose came up until the fiery streak of the tracer bullets merged with the whirling glint of the gas plane's propeller, ripped a line of flame up the belly of the criminal's ship.

The plane staggered like a drunken bird, slid off to one side, recovered, slipped again. Wentworth sought to ease the tension of his own valiant ship. Too late a ripping crack! A wing folded upward and ripped loose, crumpled by the terrific force of that long power dive and its sharp ending.

WENTWORTH JERKED loose his belt buckles, twisted about. "Out" he yelled at Ram Singh. "Bail out!"

The turbaned head nodded. The ground was dangerously near now, the plane was whirling in a lopsided flat spin toward the earth. Wentworth climbed high in his cockpit, but waited until Ram Singh put a foot upon the side and sprang out into space. There was barely time enough for the parachute to operate before Ram Singh would reach the earth.

Wentworth, hesitating that moment, to make sure that Ram Singh leaped successfully, had dropped below the minimum requirements of the 'chute! If he leaped now, ripped out the tiny bell of cloth that would yank out the big parachute, it could not possibly open in time. It might break his fall somewhat, but he was almost certainly doomed.

Wentworth did not make the attempt. Instead, watching the enemy's plane ahead burst into flame, and plunge downward, he stood upon the seat of his cockpit, made sure his feet were free, and jerked the rip cord.

The plane was not falling in a straight line, but spinning downward at an angle, still swept onward by the downward plunge of his terrific speed. That speed helped Wentworth now. It snapped open the parachute, jerked Wentworth with a sickening lurch from the cockpit.

His feet struck the tail, caught for a heart sickening instant, then jerked clear. He swung with slow, narrowing oscillation beneath the white bell of his 'chute, a scant hundred feet from the earth. The gas plane struck in flames, rebounded and exploded with a booming roar that spattered fire and black fragments over the landscape. Below him, Wentworth saw Ram Singh make a successful landing, saw the sail collapse and then his own black plane dived into a thicket.

This much Wentworth saw, then he himself was forced to bend his knees and relax his body for the shock of the landing. He spilled to the ground, sprang up slashing the parachute cords with a knife, and raced to Ram Singh. The Hindu was jogging to meet him. Wentworth waved his hands and shouted. "Run, run the other way. Gas, gas from the ship. The wind is toward us."

The Hindu turned and raced back the way he had come. But, though he ran at top speed, Wentworth swiftly overtook him and together they sped on into the night, racing across wind to escape the crawling tentacles of gas that would creep from that wrecked ship, spreading desolation and horror over whatever part of the land they touched.

Wentworth could recall no homes in the path of the gas, and the wind was freshening. The chances were it would dissipate its strength before it reached any human habitation. But they too were directly in its path. For a mile they staggered on, lungs gasping for breath, plunging through underbrush, leaping ravines, dragging with heart-rending slowness over ploughed fields, soft with the mud of recent snow.

But finally they were clear and began to circle, making their slow way back to Elkhorn. Not a car passed along the road they trudged and they were forced to travel on foot all the way. It took three hours.

Elkhorn. Its lights blazed as brightly as ever; white street lamps circled in the wind, moving eerie shadows. But the homes were dark, and—a curse ripped from Wentworth's throat— huddled, pitiful bodies spotted the street ahead! He broke into a pounding run, brought up sharply beside one, a soldier crumpled in death, his gas mask making his face hobgoblin-like, his futile rifle tossed upon the cold earth.

WENTWORTH DROPPED on his knees beside him, tugged off the disguising mask, then sat upon his heels limply staring with horror-widened eyes at the dead face. Despite the protecting mask, his face was eaten by the hell gas, its flesh dyed a sickly green.

Great Lord! A gas that masks were futile against! Wentworth reeled to his feet and stared white-faced at this desolation. Bodies everywhere upon the streets, still cold bundles of rags. He had shot down the plane, but in its mad dive, it had dropped those gas bombs which had spread this horror upon the face of the earth. He was fervently thankful that he had managed to evacuate the people before this horror had struck.

But, Lord, Lord! A mask-proof gas! A gas that laid trained troops in cold rows upon the earth! What could the millions of the cities do against this horrid threat? What could all the powers of the nation achieve to check its mad murder march across the face of the earth?

Wentworth stood staring down at the youthful face of the soldier. The greenish, death-dyed flesh glimmered in the pitiless white glare of the lights. Wentworth's mouth was thin as a knife blade. Jonathan Love was partly responsible for his early pig-headed refusal to enter into the trap which might have prevented this slaughter. Wentworth slammed across the street to an automobile whose chauffeur had collapsed dead across the wheel. He lifted the body out, covered the dead face with a hat. Springing behind the wheel then, he sent the car roaring over the boulevards to Love's home.

Up the steps he pounded with Ram Singh at his heels, crashed past the startled butler, and banged open the door into the office where the lights told him Love still was. Wentworth pounded across the room, his face white with anger. And as he advanced, Love reeled to his feet.

Crosswell was beside him. So were Reuters and Delaney. Wentworth struck his fist violently upon the desk. "You have killed three companies of men tonight, Love," he bit out. "Three companies of soldiers because of your pigheaded refusal to use common sense."

Anger burned in Love's dark eyes. "You dare to blame me! You are the one who said the attack could not come from the air. And it did. Gas bombs were dropped."

"I shot down the plane," Wentworth said.

"But too late, too late," Love stormed.

Wentworth straightened slowly. "Yes, it was too late. But at least, I cleared the town of workers."

Then the horror of the thing gripped him. "God in Heaven!" he said. "How can you fight a gas that goes through the best masks invented? As if the men did not wear them at all?"

"It is time to think about that," Love sneered. "We've got another letter from The Green Hand." He held out a paper in his bony fingers, and Wentworth seized it.

The ransom now is five million—the town Loveland. You won't be able to evacuate that. Get the money and have it ready, or Loveland will be gassed off the face of the earth.

And the signature once more was that brutal clutching green hand!

Wentworth read the letter through, put it back upon the desk, and straightened slowly. There was no smile on his face. His eyes glittered like cold ice, and the thin breath of anger rasped in his nostrils. Love was smiling, triumph on his face.

"It has you stumped, has it, Wentworth?" he jeered. "Well I—pig-headed fool as you call me—have found a way to save the city from the gas of the Green Hand!"

CHAPTER 8
THE GREEN TERROR AGAIN

JONATHAN LOVE nodded gravely, as if in confirmation of his own words. "I have discovered a way to defeat the gas."

Wentworth stared at him. Could this man actually have achieved so soon a neutralizer of the gas? Wentworth was planning to obtain organs from some of the men dead of the gas and have them analyzed by his friend and associate, Professor Brownlee, with a view to finding the kind of gas used, and, working from this, devise a means of fighting it.

But the gas attack had taken place only a few hours before, and already Love claimed a solution.

"What is this that you will use against the gas?" he asked, and his voice was quiet despite the tension within him.

"Fans," said Love.

"Fans!" Wentworth's cry was half a snort of ridicule. "Fans? That's absolutely ridiculous. Do you think that any fans large enough to protect an entire city could possibly be built? Or that if they were built, they could foil an attack of this gas?"

Love smiled confidently. He waved a hand with a grandiloquent gesture. "Men laughed at me when I first put my money into the Venus car. They laughed at my plan for mass production, at every major undertaking I have attempted. But my plans have succeeded. This, too, will succeed."

Wentworth shook his head slowly. "Have you made tests?"

Love said, "No. This time I do not need tests."

Wentworth would have laughed had the thing not been so grave. The man was ridiculous.

"Yet you're asking the hundreds of thousands in this city to trust their lives to this wild scheme," Wentworth pointed out violently. "Do you think the Governor or the police will assist you in that?"

Love drew himself up proudly. His thinness was almost ascetic, and there was a saint-like quality to his face.

"I do not ask for help," he said grandly. "My own workers will be my troops. And single handed, we will defeat this fiend of crime who has loosed this gas upon the world!"

"But in heaven's name…" Wentworth checked himself. No

use antagonizing the man, for he could be of incalculable assistance if he would. "There is something else you can do," he urged "Whatever you do with the fans, turn all your laboratories loose upon the problem of finding out what kind of gas this is and what can be done to nullify its effects."

Love smiled condescendingly. Wentworth turned from him to the others in the room, to Crosswell, to Delaney. But even in the young foreman's face was an acceptance of his employer's decision, an appearance of confidence. Wentworth looked to the others, the darkly handsome Reuters with his precise mustache and monocle, to Tremaine Smith. All seemed to assent. They seemed jubilantly confident of success. It was the magic of this man Love that he was able to sweep others with him. Only Wentworth remained obdurate.

"You are determined to go through with this mad plan?" he asked slowly. "You won't even fight in the one way that your powerful facilities permit you to?"

Love shook his head again. Wentworth shrugged, shook his head pityingly, stalked from the room, with the imperturbable Ram Singh silent at his heels.

IN THE day and night that followed, frantic work was done. At all Love's factories, huge fans were produced with the unbelievable speed his giant plants permitted. In the rest periods and lunch hours the workers, clad in green-shirted uniforms, were drilled in regimental groups, drilled in operation of the fans and in obedience.

They were unarmed; ordinary guns would be of no avail against the gas. But their morale was remarkable. Wentworth, speeding about his own work, saw them marching, cheering every mention of Love's name, apparently confident of victory.

Wentworth obtained organs from the body of a man dead of the gas and sent them by Ram Singh to Professor Brownlee. He held a long conversation over the phone with the professor, giving the circumstances and features of the gas death. He stressed the necessity of finding the nature of the gas and a substance that would nullify or neutralize it.

Brownlee promised to work night and day, and Wentworth remained on the scene of action, watching the huge fans wheeled into place about the city, scattered through its streets—watching the details of workers drill and practice with their grotesque weapons.

No further word came from the Green Hand, but the people, after the deaths in Elkhorn, were frantic. Thousands had fled the city by auto, rail and air. Many other thousands, plodding on foot, begging rides, sometimes stealing them, by force of arms, fought frantically to reach the safety of the country. But there were many thousands of others who could not leave.

They rioted in the streets, demanding protection. It was a wild, mad city. Many sought solace in drunken brawlings; others jammed churches; a great preacher announced a marathon prayer, called on the city to pray ceaselessly for deliverance until the peril had passed.

Editorials screamed in the newspapers, demanding protection by the Government, howling doom for the criminals. Three men were killed, mobbing Love's mansion, demanding that he pay the ransom.

But among Love's worker troops was no panic. He seemed to have inspired them with an unwavering zeal and courage. Some might be timorous, but they were swallowed up in the vast confidence of the majority. Even Delaney, when Wentworth talked to him, seemed swept along by the buoyant spirit.

Government experts were in the city seeking to analyze the gas from the corpses of the soldiers, seeking to manufacture masks that would keep out the deadly fumes. And over the entire scene, hung like a huge menacing cloud, the symbol of the Green Hand, its stubby cruel fingers clutching at the city, strewing the menacing tentacles of that horror of death—the gas.

ONCE MORE Wentworth planned to take up his aerial watch, but this time he would not be alone in the air. Dozens of Government craft were prepared for patrol, too. And hourly flights of them swept up from the field and prowled back and forth above the streets like watch-dogs. Pale-faced denizens of the city, unable to flee, looked up at them, but found no solace even in these swift-winged killers of the sky.

The people moved furtively through dead streets, throwing wide-eyed glances over their shoulders as if to surprise Death stalking them.

So the first day passed. And that evening, among deserted homes on the outskirts of the city, a strange thing took place. A dozen men went about tennis courts on the outskirts of the city, sprinkling them as if to prepare skating rinks, though this night was not cold enough for freezing water. No one saw their faces; no one paid them any attention, unless to wonder at the

73

casualness of men who could prepare for sports in the face of death itself, in a town where terror and horror stalked the streets.

No one saw them use small cupped nozzles, such as hardware stores sell for use of fertilizer, nozzles which contained small balls of soluble substances, which, dissolved by the water, could be scattered over lawns in summer to nourish them. Into these nozzles, the men dropped small green pellets which they took from their pockets. They colored the water green.

For hours men went over the city, scattering pounds of the green pellets dissolved in water. And finally, their work done, they vanished into the shadows.

At sun-up next morning, a green-shirted member of Love's worker troops was making the last weary round of his territory, head sagging sleepily. He passed on slow feet a tennis court, warming beneath the first red rays of the sun. And abruptly he froze in his tracks, staring with horror-widened eyes.

From the damp clay of the court, a thin greenish coil of vapor lifted a tenuous head. As the worker stared the vapor thickened and became a thick, greasy column. And now it was no longer alone. All over the court, the fog-like vapor stirred, and venomous tentacles crawled away over the shrinking earth like giant snakes—snakes whose breath meant destruction!

THE WORKER tore himself free of a paralysis of fear, raced away from the gas, blowing shrilly upon his alarm whistle. Others piped the wild warning. Sirens moaned through the streets. Instantly, throughout the city, giant fans were wheeled to face into the wind, began to whir and roar.

And Wentworth, hearing the agitation, sprang into a plane,

and sped over the city, seeking to trace the perpetrators of this new outrage.

The city was laid out like a great map below him, clusters of the worker troops looking like scurrying ants, behind the huge, bellowing fans. On all sides about the city, he saw the green vapor of death, rising, crawling through the streets. He saw the fans buffet it, tear some to shreds, and hurl it back. But he saw other fragments crawl along the walls, sneak past that barrier of air, and penetrate behind the lines of the workers.

One fan burst suddenly into flame. Its crew fled in panic. The crawling gas crept by. A rescue squad raced up with a fan mounted on a truck, and Wentworth, spiraling, watched.

The gas overwhelmed the truck, wrapped its tentacles about it. The fan roared on. The workers still labored over it. Not a man among them fell. Wentworth drew out glasses and focused them on the scene below. The men were coughing from the fumes, but here was no instant death. They did not fall screaming to the earth, and screaming, die.

It was a curious thing, but Wentworth could not tarry here. He raced on, circling the city, seeking some trace of the men who had spread this gas. He found no clue to them. What clue could he find in water sprinkled upon tennis courts?

At long last, Wentworth circled to the airport and rode back into the city. The streets were alive with people shouting and singing. It was another Armistice Day, and everywhere Love's workers were heroes, the centers of swirling crowds of people.

On every tongue was the name of Jonathan Love. Newspapers screamed his praises. Love had done what the government's experts and soldiers had failed to accomplish. With an idea that everyone branded ridiculous, he had protected the city from horrible, overwhelming death!

Wentworth shook his head. It was impossible. And he had seen one fan catch fire, had seen the gas sweep completely over a truckload of men, yet leave them alive. And the death gas in that cabin in the wood had struck instantly. Was it possible that the agitation of the fans had kept the air circulating so violently that the gas had been dissipated in strength? Wentworth frowned. He doubted it. What, then, was the answer to what he had seen?

WENTWORTH'S TAXI made slow time through the streets. People hopped upon the running boards, shouting and waving flags. Banners with Love's name daubed upon them flaunted from every window. Finally, the taxi was stopped dead. Here was a mob of a different tenor. It was angry and howled imprecations. It demanded that someone die; Wentworth, alighting from his cab and pushing on foot through the packed crowd, thought he caught the name, "Delaney."

He threw his shoulders into the task of penetrating the human barrier. Men struck at him viciously, but Wentworth merely warded the blows and bored in. Finally he reached front ranks. He was gazing at the barricaded doors of the jail. Through slots in it, guns pointed. Wentworth turned to the man next to him, shouted to make himself heard.

"What is it?"

The man stared at him. His eyes were wild, his face taut with the mass rage. "They got one of them guys that turned on the gas!"

"The hell they have!" Wentworth ejaculated.

"Yeah," cried the man. "A guy what worked for Love. Wrecked a fan."

Wentworth stared at the barricaded doors, at the vicious muzzles of guns. "Know the man's name?" he demanded.

"Delaney," yelled the man, "Delaney. Foreman at Elkhorn!"

Wentworth's frown tightened, his eyes narrowed with thought. "Jack Delaney?" he demanded.

"That's the guy!"

Wentworth jerked his gaze from those steel-armored doors. He heard shouts behind him.

"Make way for Love!"

Cheers rang. The crowd went mad with joy. And Love, ringed by a thick squad of his green-shirted workers, pushed through the crowd. His hat was off, and he was smiling and bowing. But dignity sat upon him. Dignity, and again that saint-like quality of his face became evident. He was the savior of the city, and his face showed his knowledge of that fact.

Wentworth caught his arm as he passed—and only Love's quick word prevented his being torn to pieces by the crowd which suspected his motives.

"Is this Delaney that's arrested the man who came with me to your house? Your Elkhorn foreman?" Wentworth demanded.

Love nodded, his face severe. "We found a traitor," he declared.

"And a traitor must die. I shall demand that he be executed at once. Hanged publicly."

"But, good Lord," Wentworth protested, "he can't possibly be guilty."

"He was caught red-handed," Love declaimed, "and he must die."

Wentworth clung to his arm, trying to argue with him further. The man walked on. Three workers seized Wentworth and thrust him back into the mob, a mob which turned hostility upon him with upraised clubs. A pistol cracked. Wentworth's coat jerked with the passing of the bullet. He ducked into the center of the crowd and lost himself, heard the iron doors clang behind Love.

Delaney was in there, Jack Delaney, charged with being a traitor, a member of the gang. And innocent as Wentworth felt he must be, there could be no hope for him. Love was deaf to all reason. There was no chance for justice here for Delaney, and it would be impossible for Wentworth to reach the jail. He was barred from it by a mob that would tear him to pieces if he dared to whisper of unfairness in the man who had become the city's idol, now that he had saved the people from the terror of the gas, Jonathan Love.

Jack Delaney was doomed!

CHAPTER 9
"YOU ARE THE SPIDER"

WENTWORTH REMAINED in the fringe of the crowd until Jonathan Love came out of the jail again and shouted from the steps:

"Delaney will have a fair trial tomorrow! He'll be hanged tomorrow night!"

The crowd roared. Wentworth's eyes had an ugly light in their depths. A fair trial? Bunk! But for the present he could do nothing. He went to his room, turned to the solace of his music. Rarely did the violin from which he drew such exquisite music as few concert virtuosos could equal fail to comfort him, but today the notes were tortured and slow. He longed for the mighty organ in his Fifth Avenue apartment in New York, longed for Nita's inspiration and comfort. This was a savage battle, a contest with more puzzling aspects than any he ever had faced before in his ceaseless crusades against the Underworld.

Jonathan Love, with his fool fans, battling the Green Hand and, more amazing still, winning the skirmish! Delaney, set by him to watch Reuters, had learned nothing, had set about helping Love—and landed in a cell charged with betraying the city to the murder gang. George Scott vanishing literally into the air, and that mysterious accusing phone call linking Wentworth and the Spider, a closely guarded secret whose publication would mean Wentworth's death on any one of a dozen murder charges.

Wentworth's music grew sluggish and died. He placed the violin in its case, crossed to the phone and called Nita. He could visualize her lovely face brooding over the twilight on the Hudson, its shifting mists and thousand moods visible from her apartment high in the Riverside Towers. Her Great Dane dog, Apollo, would be beside her—

Wentworth's face brightened at the music of Nita's voice over singing wires.

"Darling," he cried, "all these days I've been needing the sound of your voice. There never was another like you, loveliness. Just to hear you is an inspiration...."

"I charge you," said Battleson shrilly, "with murdering three men in the north Michigan woods!"

Nita's soft laughter interrupted him. "You're incurable, Dick," she told him. "You don't need any help I can give."

"Ah, but the music of your voice, *m'amie!*" And Wentworth lapsed into French, which, he always insisted, was the one language of the heart. Minutes later he became more practical, asked her to fly out to Loveland, visit her friend, Renee Love, and see what her soft blue eyes could find in that household.

"The answer to all this murder and crime is there, I'm sure," he told her. "And I'm convinced you'll be immune to the gas so long as you're there."

He threw back his head and laughed, vitality restored to his keen, sharp face, his gray, fine eyes alight with new hope. "You have given me the inspiration I needed, *m'amie.* Till you come then...."

He hung up slowly, and almost instantly the phone rang again. It was Professor Brownlee's genial voice that greeted him, announcing he had discovered the principal ingredient of the poison gas used by the criminals.

"It is something new," he said, "and seems to have been an offshoot of an experiment in synthetic perfumes. No mask would be proof against it, and it attacks not only the bronchial tubes and the eyes, but will even penetrate the skin, when dry. It is more deadly than yperite or the American Lewisite."

"Pretty formidable stuff, eh?" Wentworth asked.

The professor laughed dryly. "Formidable is scarcely the word for it. A thimbleful would at least knock out an entire roomful of people and kill a good number of them. It has remarkable powers of combining with the oxygen of the air to recreate itself."

Wentworth frowned thoughtfully at the dead white wall ahead of him. "Would you say it would be possible for this gas to swirl around men in the open. Men who were operating a huge fan and because of the circulation stirred up by that fan, to escape unharmed?"

The Professor's reply was positive. "It would not. The very circulation of the air would increase its poisonous qualities. The additional oxygen would combine with the gas and generate more of it."

Wentworth's thoughtful frown increased, and he described in detail the scene in the streets that day, when the gas had failed to harm Love's worker army.

Professor Brownlee snorted. "Then the gas used today was not the gas which killed the man whose viscera you sent me."

"Thank you, Professor," said Wentworth. "That confirms my suspicions."

The Professor told him then that he had a theory that because of the high oxygen content of the gas, something might be combined with it that would destroy both gases in flame.

Wentworth replied in three words. "Fine, but hurry!"

WENTWORTH STOOD staring at the wall a full minute before he turned away and crossed to a suitcase. From it he took rapidly a small kit which he strapped beneath his arms, a kit that contained a precious set of chromium steel tools that would have been the envy of any burglar. It contained also a small make-up kit for purposes of disguise—and it held the mask of the Spider.

Once Wentworth had this in place, he acted quickly. Snatching up a coat and a slender cane with a long amber handle that fitted across his hand like the hilt of a sword, he left the hotel and took a taxi to the home of Jonathan Love. The guard of workers was all about, and Wentworth had some difficulty gaining admittance. Once inside, his welcome was surprisingly warm. Crosswell strode forward and gripped his hand, his pale self-effacing secretary's countenance beaming.

"Mr. Love was afraid you got into trouble with that mob in front of the jail. He was alarmed."

"Kind of him," Wentworth murmured.

Abruptly he raised startled eyes toward the flight of formal white stairs that curved upward from the hall. A girl's voice was loud.

"I will do it," he heard her cry. "I will. He's the only one that can help him now, since father has refused."

He heard a woman's high heels beat along the upper hall, heard her gasp out. "Let me go! I will, I tell you!" And then he saw Renee.

She sped down the curving stairs, the skirts of a cerise negligee trailing back from silk-clad knees. Her hair was disordered, and her face, usually so alive with color, was pale. She ran up to Wentworth, caught his coat.

"You must do something for Jack," she said. "You must! They're going to hang him tomorrow. Father says nothing on earth can save him. But I know you can."

Wentworth put his hands on her shoulders and looked into her distraught face. Her eyes were feverishly bright and haggard circles were dark below them.

"I came here tonight," he said, "to do what I could for him, Renee. I am afraid that, short of bloodshed, your father is the only man who can free him from jail."

The girl stared unbelievingly into Wentworth's face. A little moan began in her throat. She choked it back, sinking white teeth into her lower lip.

"But—but—I know Jack couldn't do it. He couldn't be mixed up with those criminals!"

"I am inclined to doubt it myself," Wentworth said. "I'll see if I can persuade your father."

"I am afraid that is quite futile, sir," Crosswell put in. "I have been doing my humble best since Mr. Love came home. He absolutely won't listen to the possibility of Delaney's innocence."

The girl swung her piteous eyes from one man to the other.

Wentworth patted her shoulder. "Go upstairs, child," he said. "I'll do my best."

THE GIRL turned heavily and, with the hanging head and bowed shoulders of despair, went slowly up the stairs. The scarlet silk of her negligee was like fire in the shadows of the hall, but it was a sad fire, like dying embers on a deserted hearth.

Wentworth and Crosswell watched her go without words, then turned to face each other. Crosswell nodded briefly. "Come, I'll escort you into the presence." There was a slight, bitter smile on his lips.

Jonathan Love was sitting behind that rich walnut desk, like an emperor. Captains of his worker troops came to him for instructions, received them and marched out with a bristling military salute. Love did not rise when Wentworth entered, as formerly had been his custom. He did not smile. All humor and kindliness seemed to have gone out of the man.

"I'm glad to see you are still alive, Wentworth," he pronounced deliberately. "I wanted to look you up when the crowd took you away. But affairs of state called me. I could not spare the time."

Wentworth bowed with a small smile. "I appreciate your concern, and I know that only press of affairs could have prevented you from coming to my rescue. And you are right. One man's life is of small moment in such times as these."

"Yes," mused the great man, "one realizes in such times what a futile, small thing man is."

"Too small," said Wentworth, "to spoil the reputation you have acquired for fairness and merciful dealing."

Jonathan Love frowned, the gouged out lines in his austere face converging in tight radiating lines on his mouth. "I'm afraid I don't understand."

"A word from you," said Wentworth, "will save Jack Delaney. You do not have to free him. Merely delay his trial until un-prejudiced times shall be able to judge him fairly."

Love had stiffened at the mention of the name. "Do not mention him to me!" he thundered. "He is a traitor of the vilest sort, a traitor who barters human lives for money! He has been bought and paid for, and he shall suffer for it."

"Bosh!" said Wentworth. "Delaney was merely conducting an experiment for me, a dangerous experiment but one which proved its worth. If anyone is a traitor, if the blame rests upon anyone, it is upon me."

"You!" Jonathan Love stared with amazed dark eyes at Went-worth, eyes that did not understand.

"I mean," said Wentworth, "I had suspected for some time that blackmail was not the ultimate motive of these crimes, that the monster behind these mad wholesale murders aimed at other things than mere extortion. Delaney today confirmed that theory. By his brave action he has exposed a plot against the Government of the United States!"

LOVE STOOD. His face was severe. A white globed lamp, dangling from the ceiling, bathed his face in pitiless light.

"You have made statements, Wentworth, which compel me to demand an explanation."

Wentworth's smile was quiet. "Am I wrong," he asked, "or have you not volunteered to Washington the services of yourself and your army of workers in the event of further gas attacks upon any city in the country?"

Jonathan Love's eyes became incredulous. "How could you know that?" he exclaimed. "Not five minutes ago I hung up the telephone after talking with the President. You could not possibly have had word from him by now, even if he had any cause to communicate with you."

"Then it is true?" asked Wentworth.

"Naturally," said Love. "It has always been my wish to serve my country. But how did you know?"

"It is quite obvious," said Wentworth slowly. "Delaney conducted that experiment for me today. By it, he proved that the gas used against you and your worker army was non-poisonous. Professor Brownlee has already solved the problem of the gas. He knows now of what it is composed, and he is working upon a neutralizing re-agent. He says it would have been absolutely impossible for your fans to have defeated the gas!

"Furthermore, in the single instance where a fan failed and the gas overtook the men who were operating it, those men were not killed. If the gas used had been the one which was released upon Elkhorn, not a person in the city would have survived the attack!"

Jonathan Love smiled now. His face was condescending. "Preposterous," he said. "I never heard anything so ridiculous in all my life. Do you mean to tell me, Mr. Wentworth—Bah, it's absurd—"

Wentworth bit out thin words. "I know it is a terrific blow to your vanity."

Love drew himself up proudly. "Vanity! There can be no self where service to the country is concerned."

Wentworth waved a hand negligently. "There really is no use debating that. What I am telling you is that Delaney is innocent. I instructed him to make the experiment of stopping a fan."

Love strode about the desk, holding himself rigidly.

"Do you mean to tell me you were willing to risk killing scores of people, merely to test a silly theory of yours?"

Wentworth nodded gravely. "Just as ready as you were to risk the lives of thousands to test that silly fan theory of yours. I'll tell you something, Love. There's far more in this gas plot than you or most people realize. And you are the catspaw."

"I! Why, you—"

Wentworth nodded. "Yes, you. You are being built up deliberately for the role of Messiah. Tonight you did precisely what you were expected to do. Having won a victor over innocuous gas, you proceeded to offer your services to Washington.

"The next move of the criminal, the Green Hand, will be to threaten some larger city and permit you to 'save' it, meanwhile killing police and soldiers. Then it will be Washington itself. Probably together with some other cities. And they will demand ransom for the National Government. You will march on

Washington with your worker army, with the people chanting your praises in the streets. You will seize the power of Dictator, and this wily criminal, who is maneuvering you into precisely the position he wishes, will proceed to use you further, and mulct the nation of billions of dollars!

"It would be easy through special concessions from the government which you would give him, through trust agreements, through government contracts. It is a splendid racket.

"Every time your authority begins to wane, he'll merely pull another one of these fake gas attacks and you'll be a little tin god all over again!"

Love had received Wentworth's lengthy exposition at first with amazement, then with condescension, but at his final words, anger made the industrialist's sallow face livid.

CROSSWELL SPOKE pleasantly from the doorway. "Mr. Tremaine Smith and Mr. Wilhelm Reuters."

The two men strode in, and Wentworth realized for the first time that Crosswell had not been present throughout his interview with Love.

"Come in, gentlemen," said Love. He was fuming with anger. "You are about to hear me deflate this self-exaggerated person. He declares that the gas in today's attack was non-poisonous! He says that it is all part of a criminal plan to have me seize the Government! Do you think," he demanded of Wentworth, "that I could be used as catspaw in such a thing as that? Do you take me for a fool?"

Wentworth smiled at him. "Yes."

Love's bony hands knotted at his sides. It seemed for a

moment as if he would physically attack Wentworth. Smith and Reuters stepped forward excitedly, intervened with grave faces between the two men.

"Mr. Love," called Crosswell, from the door, "Chief Battleson to see you."

Wentworth's eyes narrowed. He turned slowly. Battleson bounced through the doorway with his quick jerky stride. Behind him stalked two police.

At sight of Wentworth, Battleson threw out an arm, pointing dramatically: "There he is!" he cried. His voice broke, became shrill in his excitement. "Seize him!"

The two police drew guns and spread out warily on each side of the Chief.

Wentworth smiled and shook his head sadly. "Now what?" he asked.

"I charge you," said Battleson shrilly, "with murdering three men in the North Michigan woods. One you shot and two you killed with the gas that was used to wipe out half of Elkhorn. You are the Spider—a notorious murderer!"

Wentworth stared at him. His face was still smiling, but his mind was racing frantically. He was trapped. Behind him were Tremaine Smith and Reuters, in front of him two police with drawn guns. An arrest now would be fatal. Beneath his arm was a burglar kit with his mask in it. He might be able to free himself of the charge, but a few days in jail now, at this critical moment in the history of the nation, would plunge it definitely into the grip of the Green Hand. A few days in jail, and this fool, Jonathan Love, would become Dictator of the nation by acclamation! Once established, it would be almost impossible to dislodge him. And the Green Hand would rule! He sparred for time.

"Who accuses me?" he demanded.

The Chief's voice was definitely shrill now. "George Scott, the man you tried to make me believe was tied up with these crooks you are associated with. The fact that you killed those men in the woods with gas, proves that *you, you alone, are the murderer who signs himself THE GREEN HAND.*"

CHAPTER 10
A FUTILE DISGUISE

WENTWORTH LEANED forward on his cane, resting its ferrule between his toes. "I suppose you know," he said, "that you are playing directly into the hands of the criminals? Nothing would suit them better than to throw you on a false trail, such as the arrest of Delaney and myself."

As he spoke he was twisting the grip of his cane slightly. Abruptly he jerked his right hand upward. The cane stayed between his feet but the handle came loose. Attached to it was a slender long blade of steel, a sword! The blade flashed upward, severed the wires of the ceiling light with a blinding flash of electric flame. The lights winked out. The entire house went dark. Wentworth flung himself flat upon the floor.

"Stop him! Stop him!" screamed Chief Battleson.

"Don't shoot!" Love shouted. "I'm right behind him. Don't shoot!"

"Everybody stand still," snapped out Crosswell's voice. "Then, if anyone moves—"

"Your lights, men, your lights!" Love barked.

Fumblingly the two policemen switched on their hand torches. The broad beams quested about the room. But they did not find Wentworth. He had vanished completely.

The two policemen began a scrambling quest through the house, flashing lights in corners and closets. The guard outside the house was aroused, but reported no one had left the building.

A candle was lighted in the office of Jonathan Love and he sank wearily into the chair behind his desk. Tremaine Smith and Crosswell joined in the search, but Reuters remained with his employer.

"Clever chap, this Spider, eh, what?" he remarked.

"He's a fiend," groaned Love. "Who would have guessed he had a sword in that cane? Who would have thought of his cutting the lights out that way?"

"No one else," broke in a laughing voice from the doorway, and Love and Reuters whirled, transfixed, to behold Wentworth closing the door behind him. He strode forward, sword bared in his right-hand. Love shrank back in his chair, his eyes fascinated on the point of that slim spit of steel.

"I'm warning you once more," Wentworth told him, "that you're being used as a catspaw by the Green Hand. If I thought it would accomplish anything, I would kill you. But the legend is too well built. I'm afraid you'd do a John Brown on me." Wentworth laughed shortly, "And your spirit go marching on. Mr. Reuters," he said, "I'll trouble you to accompany me."

He presented the sword point to Reuters' breast. The man's face retained its startled expression. The monocle dropped from his eye, glinting at the end of its cord.

"Backward," ordered Wentworth softly, and Reuters moved. "Open the door and keep on," said Wentworth. His left hand held the pencil flashlight now, directing its ray blindingly into Reuters' eyes. They moved out of the office, and he closed the door. Instantly Love's voice shrieked out.

"Here he is! The Spider! Here, to me!" he cried.

Wentworth caught Reuters by the collar, thrust him rapidly ahead. Through a hall and out a side door, into the garage, he hustled. Four cars were parked there, two of them limousines. Into one of these, Wentworth forced Reuters and drew the curtains.

"Strip," he ordered, briefly. Reuters gaped at him. Wentworth repeated sharply. "Take off your clothes," and emphasized his words with a prick of the sword point. Reuters' hands flew to the fastenings of his clothing.

OUTSIDE THE search for the Spider raged on. Men shouted excitedly back and forth. Feet pounded through the house. Lights threw their slashing rays about erratically. Abruptly the entire building blazed with light. The fuse had been mended and every light in the house turned on. Reuters had removed his clothing now, and Wentworth bound him hand and foot, stripped adhesive tape across his mouth. Rapidly then he donned Reuters' clothing.

93

From the kit beneath his arm he drew makeup materials, darkened his complexion. As he worked he talked lightly to his captive.

"Disguise is not nearly so difficult a thing as people believe," he said. "For instance, a man who imitated me would have to cultivate an easy swing to his shoulders, a certain stiff-necked carriage of the head and a trick of lifting the eyebrows. If he did those things correctly, and his features were even moderately like mine, he would get by.

"I fancy that you, Mr. Reuters, are notable chiefly for your monocle. With that, the mustache and a few heel clickings, I'll have no difficulty getting by." As he finished speaking, he attached a brisk mustache to his lip, screwed the monocle into his eye and gaped vacuously down at Reuters. "Clever chap, this Spider, eh, what?" he laughed and, closing the door of the limousine upon the captive Reuters, he entered the house.

A policeman sprang at him with a leveled light, and Wentworth stared at him coldly through his monocle. "I wish you'd put that thing away," he said, indicating the gun with a careless hand. "It makes me so dashed nervous."

He strolled back to the office where he had left Love and found the Savior of the Country with his arms about a woman.

Wentworth gaped at them through his monocle. "Uh," he said, "I beg your pardon. Deuced awkward of me." He turned and started out, carrying himself with the stiffly military air of Reuters.

"Quite all right," boomed Love. Wentworth turned back. "I don't know if you've ever met Olga?" Love went on.

The woman was facing Wentworth now. She was a golden blonde, with a massed pile of hair. Her black dress was a shimmering silken mold for her body. She smiled, and her mouth was pale.

"Madame Bantsoff," said Love, "may I present Herr Reuters?"

Wentworth clicked his heels and lifted her hand to his mustache.

"I just couldn't stay away," the woman said, with a slight blurry accent. "I am so excited over what Jonathan have done. I must come and tell heem."

Wentworth straightened, peering at her vacuously through his monocle. "Dashed fine thing he did," he murmured. "Not another man in the country could have equaled it."

"Eet ees what I have told heem," Madame Bantsoff said "Now he must not stop. He must go on. Washington, the whole countree, wait for heem, with arms open—so." And she spread her gorgeously warm arms in an all embracing gesture.

Wentworth retreated a pace, stammering, "I—I beg your pardon."

Madame Olga threw back her head and laughed. Her laugher was throaty and deep.

"Eet ees that you think, I make—what you call—improper proposal, eh? But no, I just show how the countree feel about my Jonathan." She turned and put her hand on Love's arm and he looked down at her, fatuously, for all the lined austerity in his face.

"I am afraid you have too good an opinion of me, my dear," he said. "But the country does make certain demands. Just now

I am engaged in the capture of a notorious murderer, called the Spider. He's still somewhere about the estate. I will leave you in Herr Reuters' protection for a few moments." He bowed gravely and went out.

He had scarcely left when the woman ran, with quick little steps to Wentworth's side and placed both her white hands upon his arm. "Oh," she moaned, "I am so afrraid of thees beeg bad Spider! But you will protect me, yes?" She turned her green half-closed eyes upon his. Her pale mouth was lifted, lips just apart….

And Wentworth—Wentworth said, emptily, "Haw—fawncy!"

He retreated from her soft hands—too close an observation might easily detect the hurried disguise he had applied.

Abruptly Crosswell dashed into the room. "The Spider! The Spider!" he cried.

The woman flung her arms convulsively about Wentworth's neck.

"Where—where?" she quivered.

The door across the room flung open, and Reuters, face angry and red, clad only in underwear, shoes and socks, strode into the room. He flung out a hand at Wentworth.

"There he is!" he shouted.

Olga Bantsoff stared from one to the other, reeled back with her hands outthrust before her. Crosswell jerked out an ugly short-barreled revolver and fired point blank at Wentworth!

CHAPTER 11
MADAME BANTSOFF

IN THE instant the revolver exploded, Wentworth's hand flew out. He knocked the muzzle fractionally aside, so that the bullet fanned harmlessly past. His right fist traveled in a short, swift arc, smacked home, and Crosswell stiffened and did a backward dive.

Wentworth snatched up Crosswell's gun, plunged through the door, circled once more to the garage, and darted out onto the driveway.

A large car was parked there, and he swiftly opened the trunk at its back, climbed in and closed the top after him.

They were cramped quarters, and Wentworth was forced to endure them for half an hour before footsteps crunched on the gravel and he heard Olga Bantsoff bid Love good-night.

The limousine surged forward then and Wentworth continued doubled within the trunk until the machine halted finally before an apartment house, whose number he spied by easing up the top of the trunk. The woman got out. The limousine pulled off.

As it turned off the tree-lined avenue into a darker side street, Wentworth climbed out, crouched upon the bumper and, when the car slowed for a turn, he dropped off, darted to the shadows of a house. The car rolled on. He hastened back to the apartment Olga Bantsoff had entered and located her quarters without difficulty.

Still disguised as Reuters, he went unannounced to her suite.

A lock pick from the tool kit beneath his arm opened the door soundlessly. He slipped in.

Rose color lights glowed in the hall. Between the heavy drapes of the doorway, he caught the subdued glow of lamps upon a luxurious divan. He could see only one end and upon its cushions rested the crossed silken ankles of a woman. Silently Wentworth moved, and the soft blue of a trailing negligee became visible, then a soft white throat and finally the face and raised arms—she had cupped her hands behind her golden head—the face of Olga Bantsoff.

A cigarette dangled from her pale lips—a long cigarette with a golden tip—and a screen of blue smoke floated before her narrowed green eyes. She was staring at the ceiling, deep in thought. Wentworth's quick glance about the balance of the draped and be-cushioned room revealed no other occupant. Parting the curtains, he stepped in.

The woman's head jerked about, her eyes flying wide. For a moment she stared at him, wildly, a hand clutching the side of the divan. Then she relaxed; her eyes and her pale mouth smiled. She held out a graceful hand.

"An unexpected pleasure, Mr. Spider, I am so glad you kept on that funny little mustache."

Wentworth sauntered across, bent over her hand with a little click of his heels.

"I could not stay away," he said.

Olga's face was serious now. Her eyes, heavy lidded and long, met his own secretively. "No," she said softly, "we have things to say to each other." One of her hands still rested in Wentworth's. The other she took now from behind her head and dropped behind her. She rolled her hips, made room for Wentworth to sit upon the divan.

Still smiling, Wentworth sat, and his left hand shot behind her, seized her wrist. Slowly he lifted her hand into view, took from her fingers an ugly, heavy-calibred derringer.

"I think I, at least, will talk more comfortably," he said pleasantly, "if I take charge of this."

HE DROPPED the weapon into his pocket. The woman's eyes glared hatred into his. Then she relaxed her stiffening body, parted her nearly bloodless lips so that her teeth gleamed. It was not a very successful smile. In it was fright, and some menace.

"I dislike," said Wentworth slowly, "to talk business with so lovely a woman, so we will get the business done with as quickly as possible. How much will you take to leave this city, go back to New York and communicate no further with our mutual friend, Jonathan Love?"

The woman's expression did not change except that her long sleepy eyelids seemed to become heavier.

"I love improper proposals," she murmured.

Wentworth's lips smiled, but his eyes were cold and unwavering.

"How much?" he repeated softly.

The woman lifted one shoulder in a delicate shrug, and the heavy silk of her blue robe dragged away from its whiteness so that its entire rounded symmetry was exposed. She did not draw the robe back into place.

"But you are so cold blood about thees," she protested. "Here you carry me off by force an' you 've no ardor, no fire!"

Wentworth's smile became saturnine. He leaned slowly toward her. His voice was cold. "How much?" he repeated.

The woman reached out a languid hand, picked up another of the long cigarettes with its golden tip from a small table at her side, placed it between her lips. Wentworth drew out the small platinum and black cigarette lighter and snapped it into flame. Olga smiled, breathing smoke, allowed her arm to drop across his knees.

Wentworth smiled back and touched the base of the lighter upon her arm's soft flesh an instant before he restored it to his pocket. The woman glanced down, choked back a scream.

Upon the whiteness of her arm glowed something crimson, a blood-red spot with horrid hairy legs—*the seal of the Spider!*

"For the last time," said Wentworth softly, "how much?"

The woman's lips snarled back from small white teeth like an angry cat. Anger caught fire in her narrowed green eyes and she caught her arm to her breast, white hand masking that vermilion seal that glowed like an angry burn upon the flesh.

"Fool!" she spat up at him, "do you think all your money could buy me?"

"All my money is quite a lot," said Wentworth. "But I wasn't offering that much to a cheap little tramp."

The woman's anger mounted. Hectic spots flushed her cheekbones.

"Tramp, am I?" Her voice was harsh; gone from it was all trace of accent. "Hy, you cheap punk, we'll rub you out—"

She broke off sharply at Wentworth's amused smile.

"Clever, aren't you?" she sneered.

Wentworth drew one of his own privately blended cigarettes from his case, snapped a light to it. "I should know that accent," he said. "Tenth Avenue, isn't it? But you do quite well, Maggie. Maggie Foley, if I'm not mistaken?

"I wonder, Maggie, how you would like me to turn in that pistol with your finger prints on it to the police here? Even in Michigan there is a penalty for firearms, and with your two previous offenses in New York, you could pull quite a heavy stretch. Finger prints don't lie."

FEAR WAS in the woman's eyes now. Fear that struggled with hate. Her tongue touched dry lips. "How much?" she asked hoarsely.

"No fair, Maggie," said Wentworth lightly. "You're stealing my question."

"How much?" she asked sharply. "How much for the gun? How much to leave me alone?" She thrust herself up from the couch on rigid arms. The rounded softness of her bared shoulder became bony with tension. Her face was inches from Wentworth's. "How much, damn you?"

Wentworth stared directly into her eyes. "Leave the city," he said coldly. "Don't communicate again with Love."

"But why, why—"

Wentworth stood slowly. "A needless question, my dear. We both know the answer." His voice rasped suddenly. "The Green Hand works through you. You are his control over Love. Through you, he hopes to rule the entire country. You are the keystone.

Get out of town, stay out and don't communicate with Love again. Or this gun goes to the police. Your record goes to Love."

The woman surged to her feet, arms rigid at her side. "He won't believe you, he won't!"

Wentworth, backing across the room, smiled coldly. "I hope that he does believe me, if you make it necessary for me to present this evidence, for otherwise I shall have to kill you."

He said it without emphasis, in the conversational tone that a man might have said, "I'll see you tomorrow." But the woman blanched. She backed up, and, the divan catching the back of her knees, she sank upon it limply. Her eyes were wide.

"You would," she said hoarsely, "you'd—really—kill—me!"

Wentworth said, "Of course. You have two hours," he said. "At the end of that time I'll return with my gun and the little red seal." His cold smile did not alter. "Don't make it necessary for me to put the seal on your forehead!"

He stepped through the curtains and was gone.

CHAPTER 12
TRAP FOR THE SPIDER

WENTWORTH CROSSED the hallway, opened and closed the door, but did not go out. He hid in a dark corner in the folds of a curtain and waited. High heels beat a muffled rush across the thick carpet within the room. Olga Bantsoff, nee Maggie Foley, swept aside the portières and darted across hall, face distorted with anger, an automatic in her hand.

She sprang to the door, grabbed the knob, halted. For a tense moment she stood there, Wentworth watching quietly from the shadows. Then she spun, and robe trailing back from the round white nakedness of her thighs, plunged back into the apartment with arms out-thrust ahead of her. Wentworth heard her gabbled half hysterical voice shouting into a telephone. "In two hours!" she cried. "In two hours he's coming back to kill me. I've got to get out of town. I—"

She broke off, and there were seconds of silence. Then she spoke again slowly. "I'm afraid," and her words were weighted with fear. Then, "All right," she said, slowly. "But hurry! For God's sake, hurry!"

Wentworth had twenty minutes more to wait Then a faint buzz sounded distantly in the apartment, and Olga rushed to the door. Hand on the knob, she hesitated once more, thrust aside a peephole cover, then jerked the door wide. Two men entered. They were slight, fastidiously overdressed in flashy clothing. Their hands were in the pockets of their coats.

Wentworth watched cold-eyed from the corner, as without a word of salutation the two stalked on into the room beyond. The woman closed the door and followed. This was not as good as Wentworth had hoped. He had thought possibly the leader himself would come to trap so important a person as the Spider, but—and Wentworth smiled thinly—the man had been too cautious, had sent his underlings to kill. Well, even underlings had tongues.

Wentworth stole forward, gun in hand. Olga was standing before the couch, rigidly, her hands knotted before her. She was talking swiftly, and fright still on her face. One of the men had pushed a low-crowned derby to the back of his head. His overcoat was unbuttoned and, back to Wentworth, he stood with hands in trouser pockets. The other man, a fresh, light felt upon his head, still had his hand upon his hidden gun.

Wentworth thrust through the curtains, "Hands up, both of you!" he clipped out. "The Spider speaking."

A small choked scream tore from Olga's throat. She jerked her hands to her face and stood motionless. The man's hands came slowly out of their pockets. Without warning, the man in the derby whirled. Flames lanced from his hand. Wentworth had caught the movement. He flung aside as lead fanned by. His own gun blazed a reply.

The head of the gunman snapped back, and the derby fell to the floor and bounced.

"Keep those hands up," Wentworth ordered. The man in the slouch had held them rigidly. The other man tried desperately to lift his revolver again. There was a startled look on his face. A red stain widened on his breast. His hand drooped. The gun fell from relaxing fingers. His head sagged forward, and pulled his entire body behind it. His body made a dull sound on the rug.

Wentworth advanced slowly into the room. The woman's arms hung lifelessly at her side. She swayed on her feet.

"No," she said, hoarsely, "No. Don't kill me. I'll go."

Wentworth ignored her. "You, punk, come here."

The man's small beady eyes glinted. He advanced slowly.

"Turn your back," ordered Wentworth and swiftly patted

Wentworth's spring from the floor was lightning
fast. He struck Olga's wrist; sent the gun spinning.

over the man's garments for weapons. He located a pistol and pressing his weapon into the small of the man's back; dipped into the right overcoat pocket for the gun. The man whirled to his left. Wentworth's wrist caught in the pocket and he was jerked off balance!

HE SLASHED out with the gun barrel, sent the torpedo reeling with a bloody gash across his head. He plunged onto the divan and Wentworth flung flat to the floor. Lead blasted by from behind, a fraction of a second too late. Olga had entered the battle!

Wentworth's spring from the floor was lightning fast. He struck Olga's wrist, sent the gun spinning. His thrust hurled Olga half across the room, so that she fell, silken legs flying in the air.

Wentworth whirled back to the man upon the divan. His gun was out and along its barrel his beady eye glinted. No chance to shoot the gun from his hand and save the man for questioning. No chance to do anything but snatch one swift shot to save his own life. Wentworth's trigger finger was a fraction ahead of the gunman's. His bullet crashed into the man's forehead. And the other's shot went wild.

Wentworth cursed savagely once. Two dead men, where he had hoped for a clue to the Green Hand. And police would be upon the building any moment.

Olga was stretched limply upon the floor. Her head had struck heavily and she was unconscious. Wentworth darted to a window, flung it up. Police cars already were parked before the apartment and a stream of blue coated men dashed for the entrance. Others spread a swift cordon and, as Wentworth watched, one sprang to the fire escape, and another took up his stand beneath it, drawn gun in hand.

Wentworth whirled back to Olga. She was raising a slow, heavy head from the floor. He crossed the room in two swift strides, stopped an instant beside the bodies of the two men and, when he had passed, the Red Seal of the Spider glowed on their foreheads!

He jerked Olga to her feet and darted from the apartment, ran swiftly down two flights of stairs, half carrying, half dragging the still semiconscious woman. A half dozen apartment doors presented their blank faces. Wentworth darted to the nearest. The door yielded almost instantly to his lockpick. Letting Olga slump to the floor, he ran swiftly into the room.

"It's the police," he shouted. "We're looking for a burglar."

Silence answered him. Wentworth plunged across the living room, his pencil light showing the way, flung open a door. The bedroom was empty. He was in luck. He darted back up the hall.

Olga was staggering toward the elevator. Wentworth seized her, clapped a hand over her mouth and dragged her into the apartment, locking the door behind him. Straight to the bathroom he carried her, jerked open the medicine cabinet. Adhesive and gauze. He stripped the adhesive tape across her mouth, effectively silencing her, snatched up the gauze and, carrying her to the other room, tumbled her upon the bed.

A pillow case shredded provided rope. He bound ankles and wrists, and with swiftly expert hands began to bandage her head. When he had finished, the gauze completely concealed her mouth, one eye and most of her face. Muffled sound came out through the gauze and tape.

Wentworth grinned coldly at her. "Keep it up," he said. "That's swell." He jerked down the covers beneath her, tucked them neatly under her chin. Her blonde hair was disordered. Her one visible eye glared wildly.

"Perfect," Wentworth told her. More sound mumbled from behind the gag. Wentworth laughed.

He crossed to a chiffonier and found pajamas. Swiftly he undressed, stacking his clothes neatly and got into the pajamas. He glanced about the room. A photo on the dressing table caught his eye, a scrawled line, "Your loving sister, Mary." Wentworth smiled. The name might prove useful. He darted to the kitchen and came back with a glass half full of water. He set it upon the table by the bed, laid over it a piece of paper on which he scribbled "One every three hours" and placed a spoon upon the paper.

From the bathroom he got a hot water bottle, filled from the faucet, and a medicine bottle with a stained label and a prescription number upon it. This also he placed upon the table—as the doorbell buzzed.

WENTWORTH DID not go immediately. His feet were slow and heavy. As he moved across the room, down the hall, his fingers rumpled his hair. His slippers clumped. And it was a man, eyes heavy with sleep, who opened the door to the police.

"Got to search your apartment," one of the two cops said

roughly. "There's a murderer loose in this house. And we got to find him."

Wentworth blinked at him. "Nobody here," he mumbled. "Nobody but me and the wife. And she's sick as hell. Got banged up in an auto accident."

"Don't make no difference," said the cop. "We got to do it."

Wentworth began to wake up. "But look here, officer, I tell you my wife is sick."

The cop shook his head stubbornly. "I know how it is," he said. "But we got to do it. We'll be quiet as possible. This guy murdered two men upstairs, and he might be hiding in your place without you knowing it."

Wentworth was indignant now. "This is an outrage," he said. "You'll scare my wife to death."

"Now, listen—" the cop began.

His companion thrust in, "Aw, bop him and go on in. We ain't got no time to argue. Listen, Mister, any more lip outa you, and you goes to jail for obstructin' police, see?"

Wentworth's white face became frightened. "All right, all right," he said. "You can come in, but if my wife suffers from this, I'm going to sue the city."

"Sue and be damned," the cop growled. He shoved past Wentworth and went in.

Their search was casual. One thrust an apologetic face into the bedroom, saw Olga bandaged and trying to get out words through her gag. He ducked out again.

"Geez, Mister," he said, "that's bad. My wife was in a crackup once."

"Aw, come on," growled the other.

The two officers made their heavy footed way to the door, jerked it open and collided with a man and a woman coming in.

"What the hell!" sputtered the man. There was a key in his right hand. He stared at the cops. These were the actual occupants of the apartment, Wentworth knew in a flash.

HE SMILED at the man delightedly, held out his hand. "Come in, come in," he said. "Mary had an accident, just around the corner from here. Auto smacked into our taxi. And you were the first ones we thought of."

"Mary!" cried the woman, startled. "Mary in an automobile accident!"

She darted down the hall past Wentworth. The man glared at him suspiciously and went in. The officers peered after them a moment, then shrugged, and went on with their search.

Wentworth closed the door, jabbed a gun into the man's back. "Keep your mouth shut," he said. "I'm not doing you any harm, but I've got to get out of this building."

"What the hell is this?" the man demanded. Wentworth smiled. It was invisible to the outraged tenant, but it was none the less merry. "I haven't quite figured it out myself," he said cheerfully, "but as soon as I do, I'll let you know."

With the prodding gun, he urged the fluttering, protesting man on into the apartment, found the woman solicitously bending over the bandaged Olga.

"Oh, I'm so sorry, dear," she was saying.

Once more Olga grunted her muffled protests through the

gag. It was excellent imitation of groans of pain. But Wentworth had no time to enjoy the scene further. Swiftly he bound the man and woman, gagged them with adhesive, and, resuming his clothes, went down the elevator.

Police stopped him in the hall. Wentworth protested angrily, waving the prescription bottle he had taken from beside the bed and emptied.

"But my wife's sick," he protested. "I've got to get medicine for her and the damn drug store won't deliver at this time of night."

The cop was stubborn. "Orders are nobody leaves this building," he said. "You don't go."

"But the police searched my apartment," Wentworth protested. "They can tell you my wife's sick and I've got to go."

"Who searched it?" the man demanded. Wentworth looked about. There were a half dozen cops in the lobby and Wentworth spotted the red face of the cop who had been solicitous. "There he is," he said, "the Sergeant over there."

"He ain't no sergeant," the man grunted. "Say, Mulvaney, this guy says his wife is sick and he's got to get medicine."

The cop slouched over. "Yeah, that's right," he said. "I saw her myself, all bandaged up like a mummy. Geez, feller," he said, "that's bad. My wife was in a crackup once."

The other cop who had stopped Wentworth, stared at him dubiously.

"Well, I reckon it's all right," he said. "But you get back here damn fast, see?"

WENTWORTH WAS smiling as he walked out of the

building, but anger burned deep within him. His plans for trapping a henchman of the Green Hand and forcing him to reveal the identity or at least a clue to the leader had failed. He had been forced to kill two men and to leave Olga behind.

Delaney, upon whose help he had counted, was in prison, undoubtedly doomed to be hanged the following day, unless Wentworth could intervene. And Olga would be heavily guarded now by Love's workers or by the gangster with whom she was allied. That point of attack was closed, too. He might check on Scott through the police, try to trace the man who had accused him to them, but first he must liberate Delaney. Then he must go to Professor Brownlee and complete his work upon the neutralizing gas. Once that was done, he could fight the Green Hand on more nearly equal terms.

Delaney first—Wentworth caught a taxi a few blocks from the apartment house. "Corner of Broad and Second," he ordered. That would take him to the vicinity of the jail. It was obvious that appeal to Love was hopeless. His only chance was to effect the escape of Delaney from the heavily armed and barricaded jail. And Wentworth did not war with police. He might defeat

Richard Wentworth

or trick them, but his guns were silenced in combat with the forces of law and order.

In an hour, dawn would be streaking the Eastern sky with gray. The night was bitter, and the taxi driver had a leather coat hunched about his ears, heavy mittens upon his hands. Wentworth grinned crookedly at the sign on the taxi window declaring in black capitals "Heated Taxi." He thrust his hands deep into his coat pockets.

The taxi's motor was loud in the deserted streets. Wind whined by shrilly. Suddenly, as they puttered along Broad past Fifth Street, other sounds burst in the still night. The chattering of machine guns! The blasting discharge of sawed off shotguns!

The taxi driver jammed on brakes, jerking sideways in a sharp skid, swung the taxi around a corner, unheeding Wentworth's sharp command to halt. The firing crescendoed behind. The taxi raced on. Wentworth jerked out his gun and jammed it against the man's neck.

"Get back to Broad Street," he ordered.

"Geez, Mister, we'll get shot if we do," the driver protested.

"You'll get shot if you don't," Wentworth snapped.

Reluctantly the driver turned back. But he killed time, despite Wentworth's orders. And when they rounded the corner of Broad the street was deserted, empty except that the bodies of two men lay sprawled there. Wentworth's swift gaze swept the avenue. His eyes stared. His voice turned hoarse in his throat.

"Get away from here fast," he shouted. "Back the way we came, into the wind."

The taxi driver gaped at him.

"Quick, man, or we die! It's the green gas!"

The green gas! Lord, yes! There it was, crawling along the street, thrusting streamers like the heads of venomous snakes into the air. Thick green coils that seemed like living predatory things, an unearthly beast, that breathed death.

The taxi whirled, bumped over the curbing, raced back down the way they had come. It nosed into the eastward wind and sped away.

It was an hour later that Wentworth heard boys screaming extras in the streets and read that Jack Delaney had escaped from jail with the help of men who had blasted their way in with machine guns and had killed all pursuers with clouds of the deadly green gas!

The Green Hand had rescued Jack Delaney!

CHAPTER 13
THE SPIDER IS CRIPPLED

WENTWORTH STARED with gray doubting eyes at the headlines which heralded this latest *coup* of the Green Hand. Was it possible that he had been mistaken in Delaney, that the man actually was implicated in the maneuvers of the Green Hand?

With a start, Wentworth realized that the redheaded foreman was the same build and general stature of the George Scott whom he had battled in that cabin in the Michigan woods and who had filed charges against him with the police of Loveland. True, Delaney had been in jail at the time of the phone call to the police, but some one else could have phoned for him. And Delaney wouldn't have known Crosswell's secret identification to phone Love's guards on the first occasion when his arrest had been ordered.

He might easily have done it when informed that a "Mr.

Wentworth" wished to see him, since apparently he knew the Spider's identity.

In addition to all this, Delaney had been away from Loveland, Wentworth had ascertained, at the time when Scott had been in the North Woods. Wentworth frowned. He found the idea incredible, yet the facts strongly pointed that way. He went to a telephone pay station nearby and called police, asking to be put in touch with George Scott in connection with the warrant against the Spider.

The sleepy desk sergeant growled at him, "Who the hell are you?"

"Crosswell," said Wentworth, "Secretary of Jonathan Love."

"I'm sorry, Mr. Crosswell, I didn't recognize your voice," the Sergeant said. "But I can't tell you a thing about Scott. He phoned that message to the Chief, said he was coming in to swear out a warrant and the Chief shot right out to your place without waiting for him. And Scott never showed up."

"I see," said Wentworth. "Thank you very much."

He hung up and went slowly to the street. That then, disposed of Scott. The man might not even be in town. If Delaney and Scott were the same man, Delaney's followers might easily have phoned the police.

That wrecking of the fan, during the gas attack, for which Wentworth had falsely assumed the responsibility in an effort to free Delaney, might easily have been part of the Green Hand's build-up for Love; part of the plot to make his men believe him invincible; to build the Messiah legend throughout the country. This escape from prison with guns and gas seemed to put the final conclusive touch upon the evidence.

Wentworth walked slowly along the cold street. He dared not return to the hotel unless he altered his disguise, in which case he could not enter his room.

An all night restaurant spilled its white light across his path and he entered, realizing abruptly that he had not eaten since noon the previous day. A newsboy was talking excitedly across the counter.

"Geez," he said, "that's three extras in an hour and a half. And this last one… Cripes! Look at de headlines."

"Give me one," Wentworth said, and rang a coin on the counter. Delaney's escape was no longer the biggest story. The headlines screamed that Cleveland had been threatened by the Green Hand! The extortionists had allowed the city only twenty-four hours to raise a ransom of ten million dollars!

Wentworth read on:

LOVE'S HELP REJECTED
Offer to Rush His Fan Troops Is Turned Down

WENTWORTH STRUCK a clenched fist upon the paper, jerked to his feet and strode out without eating. There was no time to waste. He must reach Professor Brownlee at once, find out if his work on the neutralizer for the death gas had been perfected. If Love's troops did not defend the town with their silly fans, the hell vapor of the Green Hand would be loosed upon Cleveland's hundreds of thousands, and thousands would die horribly.

117

The criminal must be caught. But first Wentworth must battle to save those thousands.

A taxi sped him to the airport. He jettisoned monocle and mustache on the way. Police might be watching there for a man disguised as Reuters. However, he left on the dark coloring that had imitated Reuters' complexion and made certain other small alterations in his appearance. For police also would be watching for Wentworth!

He got by the police guards without delay, and, phoning Ram Singh to meet him there, was flying toward Professor Brownlee's laboratory near Croton-on-Hudson within twenty minutes of reading the headlines. In the plane, Wentworth speedily removed the last of the make-up and, after that, dozed until the ship nosed down on a field near the professor's home. Wentworth climbed out quickly, nodded to the pilot and strode toward the low wide-spreading cottage of Professor Brownlee. Blue-white light gleamed in a long laboratory and Wentworth went directly there. The door was locked, but Wentworth's knock brought a light tread within. A peephole cover flicked aside and suspicious eyes behind dark glasses peered out.

Chains and locks rattled then. It was two minutes before the last clank of metal permitted the door to open, slapped brilliant light into Wentworth's eyes. He smiled and held out his hand.

"How does it go, Professor?"

"Dick! Dick!" the man's tones were excited, his movements silhouetted against the dazzle, were jerky. Wentworth entered and turned his back on the glare. It grayed the professor's alertly vital face. He was a small, excitable man, with thinning gray swept straight back from a high, knotted forehead. A Van Dyke and small mustache shot with silver of years surrounded a humorous mouth, but those dark glasses hid the Professor's eyes.

"You look tired, Dick, tired," he jabbered.

A small smile lifted Wentworth's lips. "I am a little," he said. "What's the matter with your eyes?"

"This damnable gas," the Professor said. "I've been making spectrum analyses, and these glasses clarify the lines."

"I see," said Wentworth softly. He faced the Professor while he discarded his overcoat, then turned to lay it upon a chair. On the wall hung a picture, whose dark-backed glass reflected the Professor behind him. Wentworth watched. He saw the professor's hand fly beneath his coat, saw it come out with a stubby revolver. He pointed it at Wentworth's back! Red flame streaked from the muzzle!

WENTWORTH'S DROP to the floor was lightning fast. His pistol flashed from his underarm holster, and its crack was almost simultaneous with the draw.

The Professor's small-mouthed face twisted with pain. His left hand gripped his right wrist and the gun fell from bleeding fingers.

Wentworth was up instantly, his own weapon jammed into the man's belly. A quick hand jerked the dark glasses from the Professor's eyes. The gaze that met Wentworth's was narrowed and pale blue. Professor Brownlee's eyes were black.

"I didn't think you were Brownlee," said Wentworth softly.

Nita Van Sloan

"That's the first time I ever heard of clarifying spectrum with glasses."

He dropped the glasses, his fist flashed up, caught the man on the mouth and hurled him backward. He cried out, sharply, and bringing up against the wall, cowered there still gripping his gun wrist. Wentworth struck him again. The man slumped to the floor, moaning. No word escaped his battered lips. Wentworth bent over him.

"That was just a sample," he said gently. "The next time I'll use the gun barrel. Now talk. Where is Professor Brownlee?"

The man was sitting on his feet. He bent his head over upon his knees. More moaning sounds came from his mouth, but no words. Wentworth's blow with the gun barrel tore his ear. A scream began in the man's throat. It was muffled.

"Oh, God!"

"Shall I strike again?" Wentworth asked. There was absolutely no expression in his voice. His eyes glinted as cold gray as Arctic ice. His mouth was small and rigid with anger. The man flung up his head. Blood ran in a slow ringlet from his torn ear. His mouth was puffed and bruised.

"No, God, no! I'll talk."

"Where is Professor Brownlee?"

"I don't know."

Wentworth jerked up the gun. The man cowered away, throwing up his left arm.

"I don't, I don't!" he screamed. "They kidnapped him. Took him away. Left me here to get you. But I don't know where he is. I don't!"

Wentworth still held the gun threateningly aloft.

"Where is he?" he repeated. His voice rasped.

The man began to sway from side to side, whimpering with pain. "In heaven's name, believe me," he moaned. "They took him away somewhere. To finish work on that gas he's making. But I don't know where. I swear to Heaven I don't know."

Wentworth stared down at him coldly. The man was obviously terrified. Wentworth was inclined to believe he was telling the truth.

"Who took him away?" he demanded. The man dropped his arm, turned his falsely bearded face up to Wentworth, his eyes flinching from the raised gun.

"If I tell you that, they'll kill me."

Wentworth's slow smile made the man shudder. "But not as slowly as I will," he said. "Will you talk now or—*later?*"

The man's eyes grew desperate. "Listen," he said, "I'll tell you everything I know about this. You've got me dead to rights. And I'll help you as much as I can, if you'll get me out of the country. My life won't be worth a lead slug."

Wentworth considered. He could force the man to talk. But he disliked inflicting pain, unless it was absolutely necessary. And time was precious. He nodded his head slowly.

"That's a promise," he said. "But if you don't keep your word, I'll kill you if I have to follow you to Africa to do it."

THE MAN shuddered again. "Oh, I'll tell the truth all right."

"Get going," said Wentworth coldly.

"O.K." The man lifted his right arm tenderly across his knees. His eyes winced away from the blood. "I used to be an actor," he said. "Dope got me. And a man named George Scott got a hold over me. What it was doesn't matter."

"What does George Scott look like?" Wentworth asked.

"Tall," said the false professor. "Taller than you. And bigger in the shoulders. Bristling red hair. Scar twists his mouth."

"That's enough. Go on."

The man the actor was describing could be no one but the

Scott he had fought in the woods; the man who had escaped from there, yet had continued to trail and persecute him; the man who undoubtedly was an important link in the organization of the Green Hand.

The man leaned his head back against the wall, closed his eyes. "I feel faint," he said.

Wentworth whipped out a flask and the man drained some of it eagerly. He breathed deeply. Still leaning his head against the wall he went on talking.

"I got a letter from Loveland, Michigan. It wasn't signed, but I knew who it came from. It just told me to meet the writer here—at Croton. And you know the rest. Scott promised me that if I killed you, he'd destroy the evidence he has against me and give me fifty thousand dollars." The man's eyes opened slowly and stared up into Wentworth's face. "That's all."

Window glass crashed suddenly behind Wentworth. He whirled, gun in hand. But he did not fire, although a pistol was leveled at him through the window. For the man who had the weapon wore a police uniform, and Wentworth never fired on police.

"I surrender," he shouted, throwing down his gun and flinging his hands up.

"You just saved yourself," the cop said through the window.

He threw up the sash and held the gun while his companion clambered in, a gangling man, with eyes that seemed crowded by his high cheek bones.

"Where's your pals?" he demanded.

Wentworth shook his head slowly. "You're looking for some-body else," he said.

The cop grinned, thick lips showing yellow teeth. He shook his head. "Nope," he said. "We got him."

"I'm Richard Wentworth," Wentworth explained. "This man is not Professor Brownlee. Brownlee has been kidnapped, and this man was left behind to kill me. I shot him when he tried to put a bullet in my back. And he's just confessed."

The policeman peered at the man huddled on the floor. "Baloney," he said. "I've been knowing the professor for five years."

"If you'll jerk that beard," said Wentworth, "you'll find out."

The cop crossed dubiously to the man huddled on the floor.

"Help me up," the man said weakly, "and keep your filthy hands off my face."

The cop helped up the false professor solicitously. "Geez, professor, this guy sure did beat you up. We was fooling around town tonight and somebody said as how three strangers in town was asking the way to your place. I knew you didn't never have no visitors except a few highbrows like yourself, and what I heard of these guys made me suspicious. So I comes out here."

Wentworth strode forward, snatched at the man's beard, but the cop threw up a hard arm before him, jabbed the long barrel of his gun into Wentworth's side.

"Look here, guy," he said, "one more move like that and I'll pistol whip you."

Wentworth was angry. "Damn it," he cried. "Can't you see this man has blue eyes? Professor Brownlee's eyes were black."

The cop looked dubiously back at the false professor, shook his head slowly. "He looks O.K. to me," he said.

WENTWORTH FORCED himself to calm. Useless to argue further with these men. They were convinced that this was the real Professor Brownlee and that he himself was the criminal. Wentworth turned his head toward the broken window, listening. One of the cops prowled off, searching the house for other members of the party they had seen headed for Brownlee's place.

"This man's alone," the actor said. "The others went away and left him to finish up the job. They are trying to get one of my scientific secrets away from me."

The second cop's search of the place was half-hearted. Hope sprang into Wentworth's eyes as he turned from the window. He threw back his head and began to laugh. The sound was slightly hysterical. The cop whirled and stared at him.

"What's eating you?" he growled.

Wentworth did not answer him. He threw back his head and laughed again. Reeling with apparent weakness to the wall, he put his forehead up against it, then turned about and placed his shoulders there, still laughing. "Ray, rah, Fordham," he cried. "Hold 'em, *Ram*, hold 'em. Ray Fordham! Hold it, *Ram! Sing* you sinners!"

He crouched, putting his hands on the floor. "Wait," he said, tensely. "Not yet." He broke into what sounded like gibberish to the police. The two cops stared at each other.

"Geez," one said to the other. "He's gone nuts. Maybe I'd better slug 'im."

"No," said the gangly policeman. "I'll handle him." He walked across toward Wentworth and spoke soothingly. "Listen, Napoleon," he said, "it's O.K. Your team has made a touchdown now. We can go to jail."

Wentworth looked up at him from his crouch on the floor, his eyes pulled wide. He spluttered more words.

"Honest," said the cop, "Fordham won. Come on and we'll let you play football again tomorrow."

Wentworth straightened slowly. "I want to kick the ball," he said.

"Sure," said the cop. "Sure. You can kick it all over the place. But first we've got to get a new one. Come along with us now."

The actor was staring at Wentworth with narrowed eyes. "There's some trick here," he said. "I don't know what it's all about, but that guy's no more crazy than I am."

The cop looked from the actor to Wentworth, his high cheek-boned face ludicrous with bewilderment.

"Hell," he said, "he just spilled out a lot of silly words. What trick could there be?"

The actor shook his head. "I don't know, but there's something funny. You be damn careful when we go out of here."

Wentworth still had a silly grin on his face. He stood with arms hanging motionless. "I want to kick the ball around," he insisted.

"Sure," said the cop, soothingly again. "Come on, Red Grange."

"Whee!" cried Wentworth, "I'm the galloping ghost of the gridiron."

He went out into the blackness with the police. He was thrust into the back seat of a rattling Ford, the two cops piling in, and the Professor sitting in front with one of them.

The starter whined feebly. "I got to get that battery charged," the cop muttered. The motor coughed, hesitated; coughed again and spluttered into a roar. The Ford jolted forward, clattered over frozen rough ground and, swinging into the highway, began to pick up speed.

An abrupt, sharp hiss of air and a tire blew out with a ripping explosion. The driver cursed and jammed on brakes.

"If the damn city doesn't buy me some new tires soon," he grumbled, "I'm going to quit and go back to driving a truck."

"Hurry up," said Wentworth, "I want to kick the ball."

"Aw, dry up," said the cop, climbing out laboriously.

Off to the right of the road, a gun crashed. It bellowed once, then again. The cop jerked about, snatched out his gun and dived into the shrubbery.

Wentworth, sitting beside the other cop, let him start to rise, then tripped him, and jerked up his right fist with his entire body behind it.

The cop's head snapped back, and he crumpled, out cold on the floor. Wentworth caught up his gun, struck the false professor over the head and, leaning forward, jerked off his whiskers.

"That will take care of you," he muttered. Scrambling out, he dived into the underbrush on the opposite side of the road, vanishing into the darkness.

FIVE MINUTES later, he emerged on a highway paralleling that on which they had been driving. A car was parked there. A long, low limousine, three-quarters pointed hood and powerful engine, one-quarter stream-lined tonneau. A turbaned man sat at the wheel. As Wentworth emerged from the shrubbery, he turned his head and his white teeth gleamed in a dark face.

"Good work, Ram Singh," Wentworth said. He climbed in, sank with relief into the luxurious cushions, threw back his head and laughed.

"Hold it, *Ram,*" he said. "*Singh,* you sinners," and laughed again. "I don't blame those police for thinking I was crazy."

The car purred smoothly on and Wentworth's laughter died. His face set in a grim mold. On to Cleveland. He must battle the Green Hand without the help of Professor Brownlee's neutralizer.

He picked up a speaking tube that dangled at his hand.

"Westchester airport," he told Ram Singh, "near Armonk. I've changed my plans. And fast, Ram Singh."

Speed. One hundred and fifty horsepower beneath that slim, pointed hood. A hurricane of cold air sweeping with a low hissing over the streamline of the car's specially designed body. Wentworth relaxed on the cushions and closed his eyes.

In an incredibly short time, the Lancia swung through the low wire fence about the field, and Ram Singh brought it to a halt beside the single small building. Wentworth spoke rapidly to him. "Arrange to have the car kept here. Charter a plane for Cleveland. It must be fast."

He took a small nickeled revolver from his pocket, carefully wrapped in a silk handkerchief. "Have this sent to Stanley

Kirkpatrick, commissioner of police," he said, "and tested for fingerprints. And hurry with the plane. You go with me."

As Ram Singh hurried about the tasks, Wentworth strode to a telephone and put through a call to the Love mansion in Loveland. It was early morning, but Nita would be awake. It was possible she had obtained some clue to the Green Hand which would assist him in the battle at Cleveland. Twelve of the twenty-four hours' time given the city had elapsed while he had sought futilely for Professor Brownlee's help in foiling the horror gas. If ten million ransom were not paid within another twelve hours, by six tonight, the Green Hand would loose his flesh-eating destroyer upon the city's helpless thousands.

THE CALL to Loveland went through swiftly, but the butler's suave voice informed Wentworth that Miss Van Sloan was out. Wentworth asked to speak to Crosswell, got him after a brief delay. He identified himself as an out-of-town friend of Miss van Sloan whom she had wired to get in touch with her.

Crosswell's voice showed a well-bred agitation. "I'm sorry, sir, won't you come to the house? Perhaps you can help us."

Help them! Wentworth felt a cold needle pierce his heart. Could they mean Nita was in trouble? He forced his voice to remain calm.

"Help you? What do you mean?" he asked.

"I don't like to talk about it over the phone, sir."

"Come, come, man, let me have it," Wentworth said. "Is Miss Van Sloan in trouble?"

"I don't know." Crosswell's voice was slow and heavy.

"You can't mean—" Wentworth hesitated. "Just what do you mean?"

"It's this way, sir," Crosswell said, and to Wentworth his words seemed minutes apart. "Miss van Sloan went to the city last night, expecting to return within a few hours. She did not come back. And she has not communicated with us in any way."

"In other words," said Wentworth, his voice rasping, "Miss van Sloan has disappeared."

"I hate to call it that, sir, but—"

"Where was she going in the city?"

"Just to dinner with Miss Renee, but during the meal," Crosswell explained, "she excused herself and she didn't come back."

Fear was tearing Wentworth's breast. If Nita had found some trail that pointed to the Green Hand, she would have left some way for him to follow, unless—unless she had fallen into the power of the master criminal himself!

"And where was this?" he asked.

"They went to dinner," Crosswell replied, "at the Grandleigh. Frankly, sir, I'm worried."

"Yes," said Wentworth, "yes." He hung up.

Professor Brownlee gone, a captive of the Green Hand, his secret of the neutralizing gas gone with him. And now, the largest blow of all—Nita, whose help in obtaining a clue was vital, dear Nita of the brown clustering curls and blue eyes of mystery—Nita, too, had vanished!

The clutching brutal fingers of the Green Hand had snatched his allies, were closing in upon Wentworth. They were strangling the nation. And tonight, tonight the Green Hand would strike at Cleveland, turn loose his hellish killer upon the city's thousands!

Wentworth's face was stonily without expression, but on his temple the thin white scar showed a violent, angry red. Nita was in grave peril. Professor Brownlee's life was forfeit because of his work. A swift dash to Loveland might put Wentworth on the trail to rescue them, might snatch his loved ones from the evil menace of the Green Hand. Hours were precious— minutes might make the difference between life and death. The plane was ready. In five hours, he could be in Loveland....

Wentworth's mouth compressed until a thin line of white ringed it. Always the battle between love and duty, between his love for Nita and the man who had been like a father to him, and the Spider's crusade against the Green Hand. It was two lives against the thousands who would die in Cleveland if he did not race there and persuade officials. Two lives against thousands. Loveland, and save Nita, or Cleveland, and....

Wentworth strode from the building to the plane that Ram Singh was warming up on the line. He climbed in.

"Cleveland," he ordered.

CHAPTER 14
CITY OF HORRORS

A S RAM SINGH sent the plane hurtling through the early morning toward Cleveland, Wentworth hurriedly disguised himself in the character of Rupert Barton, an inspector of Scotland Yard. The man was a complete identity and Wentworth actually carried valid credentials in that name, as a result of services to England in some notable cases. The disguise was necessary, as Wentworth was now sought on murder charges in Michigan.

He bleached his hair to golden blondeness, put small rubber-discs inside his cheeks to make them plump. Wax distended his nostrils and waterproof paint made his complexion sallow. A monocle would complete the picture. This finished to his satisfaction, he threw himself down and slept. It was noon when they reached Cleveland, delayed by a storm and head-winds.

Two soldiers with forty-fives strapped over short khaki coats strode up to him as he alighted from the plane.

"You better get right back in that plane and hop off again, sir," one advised. "This town has been threatened by the Green Hand."

Wentworth nodded gravely, eyes on the soldier's young face. "Has Jonathan Love been called in on it?" he asked.

The soldier shook his head. "We can do everything he can. Why should we call in a civilian."

Wentworth nodded again, his mouth tightening. "Please direct me to your headquarters at once."

"Can't do it, sir. You'll have to leave. Orders are no one enters the city."

"Nonsense," barked Wentworth. "I have credentials from Washington. I'm here to help fight the Green Hand."

The soldier demurred, but finally yielded and Wentworth was sped to the military headquarters in the side-car of a motorcycle. He left Ram Singh behind with orders to fly immediately to Ashtabula, a nearby town, and there await further instructions.

Everywhere along Wentworth's route soldiers paced the streets with bayonets glittering, guns aslant their shoulders. Everywhere huge fans mounted on trucks stood guard in the streets, but there was nowhere any trace of Jonathan Love's green-shirted warriors.

The motorcycle squeaked brakes before the broad steps of a hotel, and Wentworth was handed over to other guards who in turn passed him into the presence of a small man with a general's stars aglint upon his shoulders.

General Sconset peered at Wentworth with small bright eyes. "You claim credentials from Washington," he snapped. "Let's see them."

The hand General Sconset flung out demandingly was brown and knotty. The gesture was quick as a gunman throwing his weapon. Wentworth tossed a small, gold-glittering badge upon the desk. "I am in disguise," he said. "The Green Hand knows me and has sought several times to kill me."

General Sconset examined the badge carefully, handed it back to Wentworth. His face had the alertness of a terrier's. Its skin was leathery, so that the creases caused by his animated grimaces seemed in danger of cracking the flesh.

"And why are you here?" he demanded.

"To urge you to call on Jonathan Love to save the city."

Hostility glared instantly in the General's small bright eyes.

"Boloney!" he snapped. "We have everything that faker has—fans, loyal troops, better discipline."

Wentworth nodded shortly. "I agree with all that, but you don't have Jonathan Love, and that makes all the difference."

General Sconset jerked to his feet. Dark blood suffused his tanned cheeks. "Is that man God," he bellowed, "that we all have to knock our heads on the floor to him? Get out of here!" WENTWORTH SHOOK his head, smiling quietly. "Just a minute, general," he said, and when the General had ceased his tirade, he added: "It is not that Love has any power at all that you don't have. It is simply this: He is being built up as a Dictator of the country. For that reason when he is defending a city with his silly fans, non-poisonous gas is released against him. Then he is acclaimed a great man. Unless you get him here, your men and the entire city will be wiped out."

General Sconset, with angry vehemence; fist clenched on his desk, heavily demanded: "Are you telling me that Love is in league with this Green Hand?"

"No," said Wentworth patiently, "but he is controlled by the Green Hand through his mistress, a woman named Olga Bant-soff...."

A soldier guard let out a guffaw and Wentworth and General Sconset whirled on him, staring.

The man shuffled his feet. "I beg the General's pardon," he said. "That name sounded funny."

Wentworth studied the man's pasty face a moment longer, then turned back to the general. "This Green Hand doesn't care about the ransom money he's asking," he said "although he'd take it if paid. He's out to control the government of the country by having Love made Dictator by popular acclamation. He's making the people think Love is omnipotent by letting him apparently save cities threatened by the Green Hand, by wiping out every city he doesn't defend. I tell you again, the only way you can save this city from that hellish gas the Green Hand uses is by calling in Love and letting him parade again as a little tin god."

General Sconset straightened slowly. "You are a good talker," he said, "but consider this aspect. If we call in Love, we help the Green Hand. I'll be damned if I'll do it—though your theory sounds so damned wild I wouldn't act on it anyway."

Wentworth strode to the desk, slammed the flat of his hand on it. "Do you think," he demanded, "that you have any right to refuse to do anything that might save the lives of the people?"

"I'm defending this city," Sconset snapped. "Strange as it may seem, I consider myself fully as capable as Love of defending it successfully."

"But, damn it, man!" Wentworth ripped out. "Ability has nothing to do with it! Just consider Love a hostage against the Green Hand, and you'll have the right idea."

General Sconset waved an irritable, violent hand. "That's all," he said. "I'm busy."

"Listen to reason," Wentworth urged.

"That's all," snapped the little man, glowering with his bright beads of eyes. "Get out!"

Wentworth straightened slowly. "The city is doomed if you

don't call in Love," he said. "I shall appeal to Washington to have you superseded."

"Appeal and be damned!" the General howled. "But get out of here before I throw you out."

A small smile flitted across Wentworth's face. He pivoted with as much precision as any soldier and marched from the room. The pasty-faced soldier who had laughed strode after him.

"Cripes, sir," he said. "You shouldn't have used such a phony name for that woman, or you might have put it over."

WENTWORTH SAID nothing, but as he walked steadily from the building, his eyes grew narrow and calculating. There was something about this sallow youth in soldier's uniform that was familiar. He strode out into the sunlight and blinked for a moment as if dazzled by the brilliance. Actually his eyes were sweeping the street, the facade of the twelve-story building opposite, watching the shadow on the steps cast by the soldier behind him.

He saw the shadow wave an arm in a wide circle, point to Wentworth, then dart back toward the building. Wentworth instantly leaped to one side, crouched behind a column by the door, eyes keenly scanning the opposite building. He saw something small and glittering arch through the air, heard it break tinkling on the steps.

Where it had struck, a minute puff of green-sprayed upward. It expanded instantly, like some hobgoblin out of the nightmare past. It became a greasy, crawling cloud, eight feet in diameter which rolled with the wind slowly across the steps of the hotel.

Wentworth jerked a whistle from his pocket and piped a shrill warning. Other whistles caught it up instantly, and a siren at the corner groaned out, sent its eery whine rising through the warm sunlight until its shuddering wail seemed to pierce the eardrums. Wentworth still crouched behind the pillar, gun in hand.

Once more the glittering arc of a capsule of gas sped from the building across the street. Wentworth darted toward the door. He snapped a shot upward at the spot from which the capsule had been thrown. A half dozen more miniature bombs curved through the air. Their lethal puffs swelled and joined until the steps were blanketed in green fog.

Wentworth's gun blazed again, and high through the air, even above the shrilling sirens, a man screamed. A black spot in a window enlarged, then abruptly plunged downward. The gas clouds moved down the steps slowly, drifting with their own weight and the small pressure of the wind. Into the midst of the cloud, the spot, revealed now as the body of a man, dived. It struck with a sickening crunch, and instantly a pillar of fresh gas shot upward above the spot.

Wentworth had slain the bomber, and his remaining bombs had burst as he fell.

Wentworth darted back into the hotel, raced toward General Sconset's office. The soldier who had followed him to the street shouted, "Halt!" His rifle was leveled.

Wentworth shrank aside, shouldering the wall as the rifle spat flame scarcely ten feet away.

The bullet ripped a jagged tear in the masonry, and Wentworth caromed from the wall, his pistol spitting lead. His bullet stopped the rifle's second shot. The soldier showed a surprised look on his pasty face, but only for an instant. Then it had no look at all. He clattered to the floor with his rifle, dead.

The door of the office flung open, and General Sconset rushed out into the hall, his face hidden by a gas mask. He strode toward the door, but at sight of Wentworth stopped dead, hand on the revolver he had strapped at his thigh.

"The gas attack is on," Wentworth snapped out. "That soldier who laughed signaled a man in the building across the street, who then threw the bombs. The street is full of gas. I think that spots the method they're going to use. Order the whole city to take to the tall buildings. They'll be safer there because the gas is heavy. And the bombers are there. We'll have some chance of catching them."

General Sconset ripped off his mask. "Arrest that man," he barked. "He shot a soldier!"

WENTWORTH'S AUTOMATIC instantly covered the general and his staff. "I killed a traitor!" he spat out. "Will you listen to reason now and give the orders?"

Furious anger reddened the General's face. "If you're all cowards," he thundered, "I'll arrest him myself." He fumbled at the gun in his hip holster.

Wentworth smiled thinly. He liked bravery, even in fools. And he could not shoot the little general. He whirled, ran down the corridor and took a shallow stairway three steps at a time. It was the work of an instant to open a window to the rear and spring to the ground. Behind he heard the hullabaloo of the chase, even above the bedlam of the streets.

Wentworth smiled bitterly. He had sprung the attack prematurely by his demand that Love be brought in. Evidently, the Green Hand did not want him to defend the city. If the dead were piled house-deep in the streets of Cleveland, it would strengthen the demand for Jonathan Love the next time a city was threatened.

Wentworth darted from an alley, out into the main street. Frightened faces showed at windows.

"Get to the roofs!" Wentworth shouted. "The roofs! That's the only safe place!"

He found a squad of hurrying soldiers.

"The only safe place is the roofs!" he shouted at them. "The gas is heavy. Get the people to the roofs!"

The soldiers stared at him stupidly.

"Orders from headquarters," Wentworth barked.

The soldiers saluted and scattered, shouting, "To the roofs!" Three such squads of soldiers, Wentworth sent out to save the people.

He swung out into a broad street, down which people were fleeing in panic-stricken mobs, running helter-skelter. Women carrying the children struggled along with sobbing breath. Men raced with heads thrown back, chests pumping. And behind, crawling, billowing, thrusting up smelly, deadly heads of plumy green, a great cloud of gas rolled. The gust from a billowing fan struck it; tore it to shreds, hurled it upward in graceful streamers.

Gas spurted along a wall past the blast, was sucked toward the back of the fan. The screams of the soldiers rose above the bedlam. One turned and ran, hands out-thrust before him as if to pull more speed from the thin air. With his mask he seemed monstrous. A tendril of gas reached after him, sped by the gust of the fan. He plunged screaming to the pavement. He writhed in horrible agony, his cries strangely muffled by the mask. Then the gas crawled over him, and the screams stopped.

Wentworth sprang to the top of a stalled truck; "To the roofs!" he shouted. "To the roofs! That's the only safe place. The roofs!"

People gaped up at him, pale faces streaming past. A few swerved toward the buildings that lined the streets, starting upward. Doors crashed as more followed, until jams of people packed the entrances. The gas crawled on.

An auto spun a corner, charged at top speed into the crowd, the driver hurling the deadly ram of it against the barrier of humans that barred his escape. Wentworth's mouth was bitter as he fired a deliberate shot into the frantic driver's head.

A woman with a child in her arms lay sprawled in the street, half beneath the car. The gas crawled on.

Wentworth sprang from the truck, raced toward the woman. Thoughts were battling in his head. Had he the right to save this woman and child when he might be shouting the warning to hundreds of others, racing through the streets ahead of the gas until some snaking tendril embraced him in its burning, death-bearing arm?

On the other hand, had he the right not to save himself when all the future of the battle against the Green Hand rested in him? He alone knew that Professor Brownlee was in the hands of the criminals; he alone knew that Professor Brownlee knew the secret of the gas that should neutralize the green vapor.

But even as he thought these things, Wentworth scooped up the woman and child and, staggering under the double burden, raced toward the door of a tall building.

A MAN darted past. "Carry this child," Wentworth hurled at him.

The man did not even turn his head. He pounded on. Two other men pushed past; one jostling Wentworth with his shoulder, almost hurling him to the pavement.

"Halt!" Wentworth commanded. "Carry this woman and child!"

The men raced on, heedless. An old woman, limping feebly toward the doorway, turned a drawn, wrinkled face, hesitated. She came toward Wentworth.

"Here, I'll take the child."

Wentworth shook his head. "Hurry, mother, hurry," he panted at her, "or you'll be too late. I'll carry them."

The feeble old woman hurried on. Wentworth ran with the injured woman and child to a doorway. Over it, he saw words in metal, "International Broadcasting System!"

Radio. That was the answer. By radio, he could spread the warning cry of "To the roofs!" throughout the city. Loudspeakers would blare it into the streets. All over the city, radios were tuned in to await the warning of the Green Hand.

Up steep flight after flight, Wentworth made a weary way.

The race was less frantic now, and hands relieved him of the child. The woman began to regain consciousness and was able to help herself.

Wentworth hurdled steps upward, smashed into the radio offices. He found his way to a broadcasting room where a man with an excited voice was telling imaginary horrors of the gas. Wentworth's hands grasped his shoulder, hurled him aside, and instantly he was spreading far and wide over the nation, the warning which alone could save the people from the Green Hand.

"The roofs! To the roofs!"

From his place beside the microphone, Wentworth snapped orders that the broadcast be made on every wave length "Rip it wide open," he said. "Smear it over the whole range!"

Then he put the announcer to the task of broadcasting the warning, "To the roofs!"

Wentworth darted to a window, peered down into the street. A green river of death, the flesh-eating gas of the Green Hand, flowed through the streets, washed the windows of second stories and crawled on. Torn to shreds now and then by fans, it reformed its ranks in a mad Dervish whirl, and crept on, silent and murderous. Its greasy coils hid the havoc it wrought, but distantly people still fled before its advance.

Wentworth saw a mass of people trapped between two clouds of the gas, desperately flee into houses. A man climbed a pole. As if the gas were sentient and living, it snaked a tentacle upward, plunged the man screaming downward into green cotton puffs of the gas below.

Wentworth, feeling nausea stir in his vitals, turned slowly from the window. Nothing he could accomplish by venturing now into the death below. He would be asphyxiated horribly before he even reached the street. Nothing to do but keep the warning going out over the air, and wait until the deadly gas had done its fiendish work and passed on. Then the vengeance would come!

Then the Spider would take the trail that Nita and Professor Brownlee had left somewhere—would follow it to the hiding place of the Green Hand. God only knew if they were still alive, but... Wentworth's mouth twisted in a bitter smile. Let the Green Hand beware of the Spider's fangs! His hand went slowly to his vest pocket, caressed the lighter that nestled there, the lighter that held Death's calling card, *the seal of the Spider!*

CHAPTER 15
THE DEATH TRAIL

IT WAS late afternoon before Wentworth, watching from his high window, saw the green gas draw its hideous cloak from over the dead it had tortured in the streets of Cleveland, saw the gas thin into air and disappear. The dead were everywhere, soldiers in uniforms and futile masks, thousands of civilians sprawled in agonized heaps, strewn upon the asphalt like spoiled fruit dumped from a huckster's wagon.

Wentworth went slowly from the building, picked his heavy, sick-hearted way amid the dead. He stopped beside a small, twisted body in a uniform with stars glittering upon the shoulders. General Sconset already had paid for his mistake.

Wentworth's face was sharp with pain and anxiety. The few hours just past had lined his countenance as might years of suffering. The Green Hand had won another battle—and thousands had died. Wentworth shut his lips tightly and strode on.

In Loveland, he would find the trail. There Nita van Sloan had disappeared. There he would find a way to trace Professor Brownlee. If they were dead—if they, too, had been sacrificed on the altar of justice, as Wentworth had been forced to sacrifice everything in the world he held dear—then indeed there would be vengeance. *The fangs, and the seal, of the Spider!*

Wentworth pushed on to the airport. His call brought Ram Singh back from Ashtabula, and they flew immediately to Loveland. There they drove to the Grandleigh Hotel, where Nita last had been seen. But their urgent inquiries revealed nothing.

Returning to his room, Wentworth found that Ram Singh had opened a secret compartment in his suitcase and had laid out a small oiled-silk package, fitted with elastic straps. Beside it he had placed a revolver. There was a pair of shoes with thick, rubber soles ready on the floor.

Wentworth's gaze rested absently on this equipment of the Spider, and slowly his eyes changed and became like gray agate. He nodded his head slowly once, divested himself of coat and shirt and permitted Ram Singh to attach the kit of chrome steel tools in its silk case beneath his arm. When his clothing settled into place again, the bulge of the kit was inconspicuous.

His coat had been carefully built to conceal it. Wentworth picked up a black slouch hat that Ram Singh handed him, drew it down over his brow, turned toward the door.

As he stretched out his hand to the door knob, there was a sharp rapping on the panel.

Wentworth drew back his hand, jerked his head. Ram Singh strode silently across the room.

"Who is there?" he asked in his peculiar, slurred English.

"Telegram," a gruff voice called.

"No," said Wentworth softly.

It was too old a trick. The telegraph companies employed boys, not men, to deliver their messages, and that voice was that of a man, and a mature one. Besides, he had registered under the name of Rupert Barton.

He crossed swiftly to Ram Singh's side and, imitating his voice to perfection, asked "Who is it for?"

"Rupert Barton," the voice answered.

Wentworth hesitated. It was true that no one knew what name he would register under; but it also was true that Nita knew the character of Rupert Barton and knowing that a telegram so addressed would be paged through the lobby of the hotel, might have used it to communicate with him.

Wentworth strode back across the room, twisted the shade of a bright lamp so that its dazzling rays would fall into the face of whoever was outside the door. He called Ram Singh to him.

"I think," he said, softly, "that police are outside. If they are, we must get away swiftly. When I open the door, if a policeman is there—"

"*Han, Sahib.*"

THE POUNDING on the door was peremptory now.

"The corner of Broad and Second in an hour," Wentworth concluded.

"Hey, mister, don't you want this telegram?" the voice outside demanded.

"That tube has the gas in it. In precisely half
an hour this gun will go off. Then—"

Wentworth yanked open the door. Three police stood outside. Taken by surprise, they hesitated, blinking into the dazzling white light which shone in their faces. And in that second of their hesitation, Ram Singh plunged into the foremost visitor, hurling him back upon the other two.

Wentworth sprang out, thrusting his foot forward and adding

his weight to that of Ram Singh. Taken off balance, two of the officers staggered back and sprawled on the floor.

"Stop him!" a cop howled, "He's a murderer!"

Behind him a gun crashed, but the police still were blinded by that bright light. Their shots went wild. Wentworth hand-pivoted around a corner, flung upstairs for three flights, and walking slowly then, went to an elevator.

TWO MINUTES later, he was sauntering calmly across the lobby of the hotel. Upstairs, bedlam reigned. In the lobby frightened guests were on their feet staring at one another.

Wentworth stopped at the desk. "What's all the rumpus?" he asked.

"It's nothing at all, sir," the clerk said hurriedly, making soothing motions with his hands. "Someone just got frightened."

"Oh," said Wentworth, "is that all?" He smiled and walked out of the hotel.

DURING THE hour interval before he met Ram Singh, Wentworth altered his disguise so that he became a mechanic, with grease-rimmed finger nails, and a predilection for a battered cap. He acquired a room in a lodging house, as a center of operations, then met Ram Singh and told him his plans.

"We go first," he said, "to the residence of one Jack Delaney in Elkhorn. There probably will be police guards there. He shot his way out of prison yesterday, and they'll be looking for him. They've undoubtedly searched his house, but perhaps," Wentworth smiled slightly, and a false scar on his face made the grimace crooked, "perhaps we'll be able to find more than they. Follow me, Ram Singh. Keep out of sight and do nothing unless

I tell you to. Then act swiftly. I'll probably be able to find," and he laughed, recalling his football trick, "some way of communicating with you."

He slouched away, a cigarette dangling from his lips, winked deliberately at a passing girl, who jerked her head away indignantly. He climbed into a rattletrap Ford he had bought. With much complaining, but efficiently, it bore him toward Elkhorn.

He parked a block away from the apartment house in which Delaney had rooms and sauntered, with his assumed shamble, past the door. It was an apartment with an automatic elevator and no hall boy. That simplified matters, but the probability was that police would have left a plant. One or two men were most likely encamped in a neighboring apartment listening in on a hidden dictograph that would record the slightest sound in Delaney's apartment.

The venture before him, Wentworth knew, was dangerous in the extreme. Yet this was the only direct trail he had. His shambling walk took him without hesitation into the tradesman's entrance of the apartment building, and his ever-ready lockpick opened the door in a few seconds. He casually pressed the button for the automatic elevator, heard it click and whir and saw the glow beneath the button that indicated it was on its way.

Presently light dropped across the round window in the door, vertical bars contracted to the right, and he opened the door.

He knew where Delaney's rooms were, having got his address when he first had thought of the foreman's cooperation. The elevator slid upward, and Wentworth, as carelessly careful as before, slouched out into the fourth-floor corridor.

He walked directly to Delaney's apartment, picked the lock and went in. If police were there, he was merely a friend who had a key. He would be in for some questioning, but that would be all. He switched on the ray of a pencil hand torch. There was no one in the room.

Wentworth walked silently across a thick carpet until he stood in the precise middle of the floor. It took five minutes of soundless effort to locate the flat, black disc of the dictograph behind books on a shelf. A single snip of wire cutters, and it was disabled. Wentworth then went swiftly about the task of ransacking the apartment for something that might point to the hiding, place of the gang, to a possible place where Nita and Professor Brownlee might be held prisoners.

He hunted in none of the obvious places. Police would already have done that. Pictures would have been searched, stuffing of furniture canvassed thoroughly, the desk would have been sounded for secret compartments, books would have been turned leaf by leaf. Where, then, to look?

A tobacco jar on the table caught Wentworth's eye. A book end on a piano looked promising. But Wentworth's swift search revealed nothing in either. He inspected the piano approvingly, a Krakauer. Queer instrument for a man of Delaney's means, but perhaps he was a devoted musician.

A sheaf of sheet music lying on a stand bore Delaney's scrawled name. Wentworth moved back to the piano, looked at the keys. He started. A piece of paper was wedged between two of the ivories. Carefully he drew it out. There was no address and no signature. It read:

Cops have a plant in the next room. If you come here, get out fast. Headquarters in wood camp until February 17.

Until February 17. Wentworth's eyes narrowed on the slip. Was it possible that this was the means the Green Hand took for communicating with Delaney? Wentworth was dubious. Since the Green Hand had sent men to free Delaney from the jail, there seemed to be no point in communicating with him by letter. The fact that the writer knew of the plant next door was sufficient proof that the note had been put there after Delaney had escaped. And surely Delaney would not be fool enough to return to his room while police were searching for him.

There was another possibility of course. The note might have been left for some other member of the gang who had access to the room, or—Wentworth smiled thinly—assuming Delaney was innocent, it might have been left to incriminate him. Or to lead him, Wentworth, astray.

Headquarters in the North Woods until February 17. And this was the 14th. A plane could take him up there and back in three or four hours. Wentworth nodded to himself, thrust the note into his pocket and turned toward the door. It flung open, and the broad white beam of a police flashlight struck him in the eyes.

"All right, punk," a voice growled, "Keep the hands that way."

WENTWORTH BLINKED into the glare. "What the

hell do you mean by busting in like this?" he demanded. "Get out before I call a cop." He glowered angrily into the beam.

"You'll call a cop!" jeered the man with the light. "You got one, punk. I'm him!"

"You're a cop?" Wentworth was amazed. "Well, what are you doing in here then?"

The light clicked on in a floor lamp and Wentworth made out, when his eyes had become adjusted, a heavy-footed dick with a red face. He held a gun in his right hand. He was pocketing the flash.

"Don't know what I'm doing here, do you, punk?" He sauntered over. "Hey, Harry," he said conversationally, "come and see what I caught."

Wentworth twisted his head about, stared about the room and hall, a puzzled look in his eyes. The cop guffawed. "Got you puzzled, huh? Well, there's a dictograph in here, and Harry's in the next room. Hurry up, Harry, and help me go over this guy."

He waited, derby hat thrust back on his head, gun held carelessly at his side. He waited three, four, five minutes. Harry didn't come.

"What the hell," fumed the cop. His eyes narrowed. "Say, I'll bet you jimmied the dictograph."

"Who, me?" Wentworth shook his head violently. "I don't even know what a dictograph looks like."

The cop held the gun more tensely now, its muzzle leveled. He sidled toward the bookshelf where the dictograph was hidden. He groped for it with a hand behind him, eyes still on Wentworth. He dislodged a book. Two others fell to the floor with it, thumped resoundingly. It startled the cop. He jerked his eyes away for an instant, and in that instant Wentworth acted!

His right hand caught up a book end from the piano, flung it in a sweeping arc. It struck the lamp; crashed to the floor. Darkness shut down on the room. The cop's gun blazed, but Wentworth had stepped quietly aside.

He stood between the two windows now, back to the wall, and heaved the other book end. It crashed in the hallway. The cop threw a shot there, ran forward, firing again and again.

Not until the pistol clicked emptily did Wentworth step forward. He held a well-padded blackjack in his hand, and with it he cracked the detective gently on the head. The man slumped.

Wentworth heard fists pounding on a door. He darted into the hall, out of the apartment, found Ram Singh with the elevator waiting.

Wentworth nodded, smiled. "I thought for a few moments," he said, "that I might need your help. That other policeman seems to be having trouble in getting out of that other apartment."

"It is possible," Ram Singh conceded, "that someone, *Sahib*, tied the knob of his door to the knob of the door across the hall with very strong rope."

"Then someone," said Wentworth, pensively, "deserves an added bonus with his month's pay. I trust that we shall be able to locate this someone."

The two men smiled at each other in the manner of men

who understand one another and left the apartment building as Wentworth had entered, by the tradesman's entrance.

DRIVING IN the Ford, Wentworth swiftly outlined plans to Ram Singh, speaking in Hindustani so that the Hindu might understand him in more detail.

"I am flying to the woods camp that you know of," he told him. "I found a clue in Delaney's apartment which indicates that the *Missie Sahib* may be up there. I think it's a false clue and a trap." He smiled thinly. "Perhaps the Spider can steal the bait from this trap."

At the airport, Wentworth chartered a plane which he flew himself. He took off into the darkness, speeding swiftly northward. He was alone and carried magnesium flares attached to miniature parachutes with which he hoped to find a landing place. The frozen lake from which Scott had taken off would give him a landmark.

The cold was intense, but Wentworth, bundled in borrowed flying clothes, did not suffer from it. He followed railroad tracks to Wacomchic, where he had started his ten hour trek when first he had gone to investigate Professor Cather's discovery. From that point he had mushed straight north, following a compass trail. Wentworth flew now over that course and less than half an hour beyond Wacomchic spotted a lake which seemed to be that from which Scott had taken off.

There was no chance for a secret landing. If the gangsters were at the camp, Wentworth's motor must already have aroused them. If it had not, the flare, which he must use to land, would certainly give him away.

Wentworth's mouth corners lifted grimly. He would have to chance it. He kicked the release and dropped a flare. Its blue-white brilliance spilled over the ground below, scintillating from crystalline snow and Wentworth sent his plane downward in a swift spiral, and took the ice in a perfect landing before the flare had extinguished itself.

He cut the ignition and for moments sat waiting in the cockpit. The plane rested in the middle of the lake, white barren space on all sides. Wentworth, still half blinded by the brilliance of the magnesium flare, his ears singing with the constant throb of the motors, sat and waited. He waited until his eyes became accustomed to the dark, until, with a sudden pop, his hearing cleared, then he dropped to the ground.

The sudden silence of the motor emphasized the deep quiet of the night. A slight, cold wind stirred, sent icy particles scurrying with a metallic whisper across the ice. Still no indication of life from the shore, no light from the woods camp a half mile away. Wentworth was disheartened. Apparently he had been deliberately tricked into a long, useless trip, lured away from Loveland, possibly because some major enterprise impended there.

But it would be ridiculous to leave without a search. Wentworth shifted his gun to the pocket of his leather coat, and moved, sure footed, across the slippery ice, heading in a direct line for the camp a half mile away. But there was still no sound from the night, except the scurrying whisper of frozen snow upon the ice.

THE WIND freshened stabbing icy points of cold into

There was a violent puff of flame, blazing instantly into an
intolerable white heat. Then Wentworth had swept past.

157

Wentworth's face. He bowed his head and strode on. Shrubbery that in summer thrust tender green fingers into the water, clattered. A bunch of dead sticks rattled in the wind. At the lake edge beeches in a frozen marsh clustered thick. Through them Wentworth battled his way. A beech sprout, an inch through, frozen solid by the cold, snapped off as he pushed by. Brittle branches rattled and cracked. Snow was knee deep.

He toiled laboriously on, climbed heavily the steep slope that ran from the lake to the lumber camp. The cabins seemed deserted. No trace of wood smoke in the air, but the wind was behind him now, would sweep away all the scent. Doggedly Wentworth went on. The first of the cabins was only fifty feet away now. Wentworth approached it slowly on soundless feet.

Then, without warning, the door of the cabin flung open. No one showed there, but light streamed out, outlining Wentworth vividly against the snow.

"Welcome, Spider," a man's voice jeered. He strode forward with leveled gun, a tall man with wide shoulders, and lamplight glinted redly on his hair. Another approached from the opposite side.

Wentworth's hand was on the gun in his pocket. One of those men he could remove. He stood a chance to even it off with the other. But if he failed, there were Nita, and Professor Brownlee, captives. And the world would be helpless to defeat the domination of the dread Green Hand.

Wentworth doubted that even the death of the leader—assuming the red-head who now confronted him with a gun was the leader—would stay the terrible massacres of the people by this ruthless gang of extortionists.

Wentworth did not fire. Instead he walked slowly toward the leveled guns.

"Hello, Scott," he said. "I rather thought I'd find you here."

The man jeered at him. "Glad to have been in your thoughts," he said, and moved around behind Wentworth. Instantly a heavy blow crashed upon Wentworth's head, and he went down upon the icy snow with a red blaze of fire in his brain, dazzling fire that faded into the soft blackness of unconsciousness.

HE REGAINED his senses sluggishly, battling a numbing pain in his brain. He moved his hands feebly, felt the bite of ropes upon his wrists and heard hooting laughter. He forced his eyes open.

Yellow light stabbed pain into them. He squinted against the dazzle, peered upward into a face that bent over his. It was a woman's face, a face with hating green eyes, with thin pale lips that twisted with mocking words.

Wentworth forced the corners of his mouth to lift in a small smile. "Hello, Maggie;" he said. "Good to see you again."

"Like hell it is," the woman who called herself Olga Bantsoff jeered at him. "You won't think so when I get through with you and that doll-faced girl friend of yours."

Wentworth turned his head wearily. "Take your face away," he said. "I'm sick of looking at it."

The woman snarled like an enraged cat, struck her hand into Wentworth's face. Long nails ripped his cheek.

"That'll do, Maggie," Scott's voice boomed in the distance.

The woman's nails raked Wentworth's face again. She jerked backward sharply.

"I said, that'll do," Scott's voice repeated quietly.

Wentworth saw that the man's heavy fingers bit into her shoulders, had yanked her back from where she crouched over him.

Wentworth was fully conscious now, though his head throbbed painfully. He stared about the small cabin in which he was imprisoned. Scott was there, with his scar-ugly face and the woman Maggie and another man he did not know, a pasty-faced chap with a gun in his hand.

"Let's get going," said Scott. He gave Maggie a shove. "You keep your mitts off of him, see?" He crossed to Wentworth, seized him by the hair and tugged him to his feet.

Waves of hot agony swept over Wentworth; nausea prodded dully at his stomach. He reeled and would have fallen except that his shoulder lodged against the log wall and steadied him. He stood with head hanging, and Scott jabbed his back with a gun.

"Quit stalling," he said roughly. He jerked open a door and thrust Wentworth out.

The frigid air completed his recovery. And though he reeled and staggered before the prodding of the giant redhead, he was gaining strength every moment. They marched up the line of cabins.

"All right, turn in there," Scott ordered.

Wentworth reeled past, and Scott's heavy hand reached out, caught his shoulder, yanked him back and whirled him through the dark doorway. He tripped over the sill, tried to catch himself and plunged headlong to the earthen floor.

A woman cried out. A man protested vehemently. And, looking up as a lamp was lighted, Wentworth's bleared eyes beheld Professor Brownlee, slumped against the far wall, then they fastened upon Nita's lovely face with its clustering brown curls and tender eyes of blue. They held hate now as they burned up at Scott.

"You beast," she cried out, "kicking a helpless man!"

Scott's rough laughter rang in the room.

"What's the difference?" he demanded "He won't suffer long."

He caught Wentworth by the collar, hauled him half strangling across the room and roped him to the log wall. He caught up a broken tree branch from the floor, and bending Wentworth over so that his bound arms hugged his doubled up legs, he thrust the stick under his knees so that Wentworth's arms were pinned in that position. He crossed to Professor Brownlee and secured him the same way, then turned toward Nita.

Olga burst into the cabin. "Listen," she said, "if anybody ties up the girl, it's going to be me."

Scott turned a broadly grinning face toward her. "I'll be gentle with her, Maggie."

The woman snatched the branch from his hands. "I know damned well you will," she snarled.

Scott threw back his head and laughed. And Maggie crossed to where Nita lay bound upon the floor.

"Sit up, you little tramp, or I'll yank you up by that kinky hair of yours," she snarled.

WENTWORTH'S EYES were cold points of rage. "Remember what I told you, Maggie," he said softly. "You harm her and I'll take back my promise to let you live."

The woman turned a hate-distorted face. "You're in a swell fix to promise anybody anything, Mr. Spider," she sneered. "Hell, you can't even move a finger."

Wentworth smiled crookedly. "Nevertheless," he said, "I tell you that if you harm her, you will not live a week."

"Hurry up," Scott broke in, impatiently, "or I'll tie up the dame myself. Don't waste any more time gabbing with that guy. He's so near the grave that what he says doesn't make any difference." He barked a short laugh. "It ain't the grave exactly, but he won't know the difference."

The woman stooped over Nita, who now had struggled to a sitting position. Maggie yanked up the skirt of Nita's dark woolen dress and jabbed a rough branch under her doubled knees. Nita's teeth bit into her lip as she choked back a cry at the pain as the branch tore her flesh.

The woman laughed at her sneeringly. "Don't like it, do you, doll face? Don't worry. It won't hurt long." She turned and swaggered toward Scott, who was grinning at Nita, eyes feasting on her dishevelment.

"I warned you," said Wentworth quietly. "That's your finish, Maggie Foley."

The woman turned toward him. Her face, with its pale mocking lips, still lovely despite its hatred. She laughed, but said nothing at all, then swaggered out into the darkness.

"Call me when you get ready to go," she told Scott. "I want to see the little toy you leave for them to play with."

Scott grunted. "Oh, get out!" he snapped.

Then from a corner he lifted a test tube plugged with wax. It was green, and the lamp light glittered on it venomously. He placed the test tube in a rack on one end of the table, then picked up a ready-made rest into which he locked a rifle, its muzzle almost against the test-tube. Next he placed two batteries, a clock and some wiring on the table.

As he worked over them, attaching clock and wires to the rifle, he looked across at Wentworth apologetically. "It's a rather elaborate set-up," he said. "It would be much simpler just to shoot you. But I have some scores to settle with you, Spider. You killed off some of my best men. You made that fool, Jonathan Love, difficult to handle. And you hampered my work by driving Maggie here from town. So you're going to suffer a bit before you die, Spider—you and this foolish professor, and the girl friend.

"That tube has the gas in it. In precisely half an hour, this gun will go off, smash the tube and spread the gas over the room. You know what happens then, don't you, Spider?"

Scott laughed shortly, finished his adjustment of the wires and turned to look at Wentworth. His head thrust forward, and gloating came into his eyes.

Wentworth studied his face carefully. Were this man and Delaney one and the same? It was possible. The general conformation of their faces was the same, the color of the eyes and their build checked.

The alterations of the face Wentworth himself could easily have accomplished with a make-up kit. There was something palpably false about Scott. There were portions of his face which were not mobile, indicting that it was built up falsely. That mouth-distorting scar—Wentworth smiled slower.

"Do you think that you can get away with this? Do you think that I don't know your true identity or that, knowing it, I have failed to take into account the possibilities that I might be killed?"

Scott's breath hissed in sharply. "What do you mean?"

"I mean," said Wentworth, softly, "that if there ever was a George Scott, you are not he. Your make-up is clever, but I, too, know something about the art. I know this face of yours is not the real one. That you are masquerading."

SCOTT FORCED a laugh. "So what are you going to do about it?"

"Before I left Loveland," Wentworth said, "I wrote out a statement of all I know about the Green Hand. It will be enough to hang you. And if I don't reappear in Loveland within twelve hours that information will be given to the authorities at Washington."

"Very clever, Spider," said Scott, slowly, but there was a sneer in his voice; "It so happens, however, that I know you are lying. You have been under surveillance every moment you were in town, and you have not communicated with anyone or even mailed a letter. I would have killed you, but I knew you'd walk into the trap and give me an opportunity to enjoy your death.

No, it won't work this time. The Green Hand will go marching on."

His voice grew triumphant. "Cities shall fall under my power, and the Government of the United States itself cannot stand against me." He walked toward Wentworth, tapped his hand against his chest. "I, I shall rule," he said. "And the great Jonathan Love shall be my puppet!"

Wentworth laughed at him, laughed long and loud. And the man crouched closer, clutching hands reaching out for his captive's throat. His eyes glared wildly. But even as his fingers closed about the helpless Spider's throat, he checked, shook his head sharply and jerked his hands away.

"No," he said, and grinned slyly, "not that way. You must live to see your sweetheart suffer, see your friend suffer from the flesh eater. Then you yourself shall die. You will notice I have placed you farthest from the table. The gas moves slowly. It will reach you last."

He turned, and Maggie Foley stood in the doorway, a woolen cap drawn down over the pile of blonde hair. The two looked at each other and smiled. Scott turned back to Wentworth, pointed toward the clock. The hands stood at half past ten.

"When those hands reach eleven," he said, "the gun will explode, and the great gas will crawl across the floor."

He threw back his head and laughed until the cabin rang with his mirth until the woman Maggie reached out and caught him by the arm with fright in her eyes.

Scott sobered suddenly. Stared at Wentworth with venomous eyes. "At eleven," he said, "you die. I hope you enjoy your wait."

He shut the door violently and left Wentworth to stare at the crawling hands of the clock, the clock that would bring death to Nita, to Brownlee and to himself, death in a horrible, screaming agony.

CHAPTER 16
DEATH KEEPS WATCH

WENTWORTH TORE his eyes from the face of the clock that was ticking off the seconds to their doom and smiled wryly across at Nita.

"You're a little pale, darling," he said. His words were trivial but there was a world of tenderness in his voice.

Professor Brownlee snorted. "Why wouldn't she be?" he demanded.

Nita's eyes sought Wentworth's. She tried twice to smile before she forced her mouth corners up. "You don't look so well yourself, Dick. You haven't been taking proper care of yourself while you've been away from me."

Wentworth shook his head. "Things never go right when I'm away from you."

Professor Brownlee threw back his head and laughed a bit wildly. There were haggard circles beneath his eyes. "Death doesn't worry you, does it, Dick? You two talk as casually as if you were in the drawing room of your penthouse. And yet death, and a damned disagreeable one, is only a few minutes away." He looked at the clock. "Twenty-six minutes away."

Wentworth turned his gaze on the professor. "Worried about this little device Scott rigged up to divert us?"

Brownlee nodded with exaggerated gravity, "Strange as it may seem to you, I am a bit worried. You've undoubtedly got some trick up your sleeve, but I'd feel much easier in my mind if you got busy and used it."

Nita's smile was brave. "Is there a way out, Dick? I don't see any with your hands tied up like that. You can hardly move a finger."

Wentworth's eyes had been casting about the room while he talked, taking in the rifle in its rest, that waiting poisonous gas, the positions of Nita and the professor. Nita was nearest that green vial. If it were smashed, its biting fumes would reach her soft white flesh first of all. And, as Nita had said, Wentworth was bound so he could scarcely move a finger.

"I have two tricks," he said slowly, "but I'm afraid neither one will be of any help. Ram Singh followed me by plane, but he is under orders to land at a distance and come afoot. I landed close by to keep attention riveted on myself and permit him to land unobserved. I think Ram Singh will arrive too late."

Nita's smile stiffened, but resolutely she clung to it.

Professor Brownlee let his gray-bearded chin sag forward on his chest. "Then there is no hope," he said. "No hope for us or for the world. Without my neutralizer, without you to fight them, the gang of the Green Hand will rule the world. Professor Cather did not exaggerate the potency of this gas." He raised his gaze to Wentworth. "I perfected that second gas, the neutralizer. But the last atom of it was taken away from me early today. If I had a small test tube of it, I could save us. The instant my gas comes in contact with that other, the two burst into flame."

Nita laughed. There was a shrill edge to her voice. "If you had the gas," she mocked, "and if one of us had a knife, if that rifle were empty—" She laughed again. Her voice became brittle.

"Stop it, Nita," Wentworth said quietly. "You're getting hysterical. Pull yourself out of it."

Nita bit her lip. Sobs rose in her throat and forced themselves out, drily.

Professor Brownlee stared moodily at the clock. "Sixteen minutes to go," he said.

"That will be enough," Wentworth cried, suddenly. "I've found a way out. Even if my second trick won't work."

"Your second trick," Brownlee demanded.

"Yes," said Wentworth. "There's a small pistol built into the sole of one of these shoes. It gives me one shot in extremity. But its a hard thing to aim accurately, and I might very well miss. But now, it won't be necessary to trust to it."

Nita raised her head eagerly. "What, oh what is it?"

"Just watch me," said Wentworth. He shot a quick glance at the clock. Fourteen minutes left, fourteen minutes before that rifle discharges and releases horrible death into the room.

Wentworth inched himself about, working so that the stick which had been jammed beneath his knees came opposite a space between two logs where the clay chinking had fallen out. He gripped the stick tightly between his calves and thighs and whirled himself, jamming the end of the branch into the chink.

Slowly, he began to tug. The branch slid an inch to one side beneath his knees before its end pulled out of the chink. But at least it had moved! There was hope!

Wentworth jammed the branch in again and repeated the process. Slowly, a fraction of an inch at a time, the stick was dislodged from beneath his knees, until straining his legs close against his body, flexing his elbows, he managed to lift one elbow over the end of the stick. It fell to the ground and though Wentworth's wrists still were bound together, he could use hands and arms as a unit. And his position was no longer cramped.

Wentworth stared at the clock. It had taken him eleven minutes to pull the stick loose. Only three remained before the rifle would discharge. No time now to saw loose the ropes as he had intended! He picked up the stick in both hands and aiming carefully, hurled it with all his force against the rifle barrel. It struck fairly, forced the rifle barrel aside, perhaps two inches.

It no longer pointed at the vial of gas. But Wentworth staring at it, felt his face grow pale, felt the thin scar on his temple throb with leaping blood. His lips closed grimly, and frantically he tore at the fastenings of a shoe. For now the rifle pointed directly at Nita, and Nita was roped to the wall so that she cold not move from the path of the bullet!

IN TWO minutes the gun would discharge, sending its tearing leaden pellet crashing into that lovely body. Nita's eyes widened as she stared into the black muzzle of the rifle, but now there was no hysteria in her. She looked across at Wentworth and smiled.

"At any rate," she said, "you will go free. You can save the country from this band of murderers. That is your duty."

Brownlee's face was haggard with fear. "Good Lord, Wentworth, do something," he begged.

Wentworth tore off the shoe, threw up both hands and flung it with all his strength. It struck the rifle glancingly, clattered to the floor. The barrel did not move. It's muzzle still pointed at Nita's head. And the hands of the clock pointed to one minute of eleven. One minute more before the rifle would discharge!

Desperately Wentworth ripped off his other shoe. This one contained the hidden pistol…. He jerked it to the level of his eye, sighting along the sole. Fifteen seconds ticked by. Fifteen of the last forty-five. Wentworth held his breath. He must be terribly certain of his aim.

Professor Brownlee closed his eyes and lifted his face. His lips moved silently. Nita still stared into the muzzle of the rifle. After that last effort of Wentworth's she had given up. Her face was pale, but there was no panic in it.

"Good bye, Dick," she said quietly.

A muffled explosion filled the cabin with clapping echoes!

A cry wrenched from Professor Brownlee's lips. Nita went limp in her bonds, her head sagged forward. Wentworth took the shoe down slowly from before his face. The smile on his lips was strained.

"God in Heaven," moaned Brownlee, "why did she have to die?"

"Look at the clock," said Wentworth, quietly. Brownlee stared at him without comprehension. "At the clock, not at me," said Wentworth, and finally the Professor turned his head about and stared at the clock. The wire which had been fastened to it, to connect it with the battery and discharge the gun, was snapped loose and still vibrated in the air. The hands of the clock registered eleven, the hour set for their doom.

"That was not the rifle you heard, Professor, but the gun in my shoe," said Wentworth. "I shot the wire loose at the last second."

"But Nita," cried Brownlee, staring at the relaxed form of the girl.

"Nita," said Wentworth, "has fainted."

"Nita," called Brownlee, wildly, "Nita!"

"Don't, Professor," Wentworth said. "I want her to be free of her bonds when she comes around."

His hands found the kit beneath his arm, extracted a steel chisel with which he rapidly severed the ropes that held him. He sprang to Nita's side, cut her bonds, removed the cruel stick that had torn her flesh and cushioned her head in his arms. Then he pressed his lips to hers.

A footstep outside the door! Wentworth sprang to the rifle on the table, caught it up and leveled it. The latch bar lifted slowly. The door swung wide, and Wentworth, the gun held rigidly, relaxed and smiled.

"Come in, Ram Singh," he said. "You are just in time to cut Professor Brownlee free."

WENTWORTH TURNED back to Nita. She came to

with a little moan, stared up into his face. He smiled tenderly at her.

"It's all right, darling," he said. "I managed to shoot the wires loose just in time."

The girl closed her eyes, opened them again slowly, then faintly returned his smile.

"I thought, for just a minute that I was dead, and…" she broke off, struggled to sit up. Wentworth assisted her to her feet.

She let out a little cry of pain, touched the backs of her knees tenderly.

"That woman!" she exclaimed.

Wentworth's face was grim and unsmiling. "She'll pay for it, darling."

Professor Brownlee was free now and hobbled across to Nita's side. Wentworth left her in his care, laced his shoes and picking up the vial of gas slid it into his pocket.

"Mr. Scott has very kindly given up his fingerprints," he said grimly.

Then the four struck out for the plane Ram Singh had landed at a distance of two miles. It was a bitter cold trek. Nita and Brownlee, enfeebled by long confinement in bonds, were forced to travel slowly. But at last they made the plane and clambered in. It was a cabin ship, with a forward cockpit that had a removable, transparent cover. Wentworth punched the compression starter and set the motor roaring.

The frigid air had chilled the engine, and Wentworth shoving back the cover of the cockpit scanned the skies while he warmed up for the take-off. Abruptly, Wentworth wrenched about in his seat, stared up into the cold arc of the heavens. A small plane was diving toward them, and he could see the thin flicker of flame from machine gun muzzles behind its propeller. He jerked back the throttle, sent their own plane skimming across the snowy waste.

They were within a hundred and fifty feet of the forest. The motor was still cold and choked and spluttered as it fought to take fuel. Tracer bullets ripped past, a fiery streak in the blackness of the night. Professor Brownlee crouched tensely at Wentworth's shoulder.

"You can't make it, Dick," he shouted. "If you do manage to take off before we hit those trees, that plane will fill us full of lead before we've climbed a hundred feet."

But Wentworth apparently was not trying to take off. He kicked the rudder from side to side, made the plane wobble crazily. Bullets scoured the snow all about them gouging up little white piles. A few plucked through the metal and cloth of the cabin itself, but none struck a vital spot. No one was hurt.

Straight toward the trees Wentworth headed his ship. The rutted trace of a wood road writhed out of the forest, made its shallow course across the clearing where Ram Singh had set down the plane. Directly for that opening Wentworth headed.

"Get back to the rear!" he shouted. "Brownlee, Ram Singh, Nita, all of you! Get in the tail!"

With a scrambling rush, the three raced to the end of the plane, Ram Singh crawling back into the baggage compartment.

Scarcely had they taken their positions, when Wentworth

sent the plane crashing between two huge trees that stood on either side of the wood road.

The wings were cut off as if cut by a gigantic knife. Fragments slammed back against the cabin of the plane, but the crash scarcely checked the speed of the ship. Held down by the weight in her tail, she did not nose over.

TREES OVERHEAD arched sheltering boughs now. Bullets could still clip through, but the trundling ship on the ground would make a difficult target on the shadow-checkered earth. Wentworth slowed the mad rush of the plane. Its heavy tires bounded over the rutted road, bounced over a ravine.

Above the throttled roar of the motor, Wentworth called back. "You can take your seats now." And as Nita walked up behind him and placed her hand on his shoulder, he turned up his head and laughed at her.

"How do you like the new limousine?"

She smiled down at him. Her hand caressed his hair. Wentworth trundled the plane at slow speed along the road. It twisted and turned, but with some maneuvering Wentworth was able to keep the ship plunging on through the darkness. He rigged a flashlight to pick out a path for him and settled down to driving the ship to Wacomchic.

It was tedious work, but several times more rapid than walking would have been. Each time they came to a clearing they must bolt across it with motor roaring to escape the bullet-spraying dives of the ship that still circled overhead. After an hour, Wentworth leaned forward and extinguished the flashlight whose uncertain light was guiding them through the woods.

Ahead, bathed in moonlight, was a wide expanse of treeless snow, a field fully half a mile across. Above it the plane with its machine guns waited.

Wentworth halted the ship and let it stand with motor idling while he pulled aside the cover of the forward cockpit and stood erect, searching the opposite woodland for the break that would mark the opening of the road. He found it at last and dropping behind the wheel, jerked the throttle wide. The plane fought the snow, finally lunged forward and, gaining speed as it skipped into the open, hacked its tail free of the ground.

Even with the stubs of wings that were left, the plane seemed ready to leap free of the ground. It struck a log and made a long bound forward.

With its tail in the air, the plane was easy to steer. It could be thrown in sharp eccentric turns. And Wentworth whirled and dodged across the open field, zigzagging, apparently without purpose, but actually heading gradually toward the opening of the road in the woods beyond.

He kept a keen watch on the plane overhead, and each time it dived, with flickering machine guns, he yanked his ship aside in time to dodge the leaden spray.

The flier overhead was working to keep Wentworth from reaching the safety of the woods. But Wentworth out-maneuvered him, sent the ship charging into the woods' road and the protection of the trees. He cut the motor, leaned forward to switch on the hand torch that served as a headlight.

CRRAAASH!!

Guns roared ahead of them, and to each side of the road,

fully a half dozen of them. Lead tore through the fragile sides of the cabin. A bullet tipped off Wentworth's seat and sang off into the distance.

Wentworth jerked at the throttle, then checked sharply. A huge tree had been felled across the road, completely blocking it!

To charge into that would be fatal. To remain here meant death, too. The firing redoubled!

CHAPTER 17
ON TO WASHINGTON

RAM SINGH'S revolver was spitting a fiery answer into the darkness. But the men in ambush were well hidden. They had only to continue their firing long enough to riddle the body of the ship and they would kill everyone in it.

Wentworth yanked open the roof of the cockpit. He jammed both feet on the brakes, stepped the motor up as high as he dared. His hand dipped into his pocket, came out with a small green vial that glistened in the moonlight. He flung it high and to the left.

Instantly he released the brakes, let the plane plunge almost against the tree that blocked the road twenty-five feet ahead, then jammed on the brakes again, at the same time jerking the throttle wide and jamming the stick forward to keep the craft flat upon the ground.

He kept the motor roaring, but even above its full-throated bellow came the agonized screams of men in horrible torture.

The screams lasted but a moment, then died into strangling cries. And Wentworth, thrusting his head up into the slip-stream of the propeller, saw great spreading tentacles of green gas, writhing about in the shrubbery behind as if the gas were a living beast of prey seeking out victims in the black night.

Brownlee's hand gripped his arm. "Dick, in heaven's name, you didn't loose that gas!"

"I did." Wentworth called back, grimly. "We're nosed into the wind. You could tell that by the way the plane kicked over the field. And with this propeller to keep the air clean along the sides of the ship, I don't believe we're in any serious danger."

For half an hour, while the motor roared, Wentworth watched the long arms of the gas drift away into the distance and thin into the air. Finally, when it was safe, he climbed down and inspected the tree that was jammed across the road. He drew from the kit beneath his arm a bit of silken cord—a spider web the Press had called it. It seemed as fragile as a spider web, yet would test at seven hundred pounds.

With a double strand of this, he and Ram Singh rigged a harness for themselves and, after back-breaking effort, dragged the tree from the path. Then Wentworth sent the plane racing on down the road, which, improving now, shot them swiftly into Wacomchic.

The town was dead, windows dark, not a soul abroad, except a stray dog that yapped excitedly, turned tail and ran as Wentworth drew the laboring plane to a halt at the railroad station.

Wentworth routed out the station agent, got to a telephone and finally awakened a disgruntled operator. He ordered a plane sent to them immediately, then put a call through to Stanley Kirkpatrick, police commissioner of New York City.

After a ten minute delay, he heard Kirkpatrick's precise tones.

Wentworth gripped the phone excitedly. "Wentworth speaking," he said. "What's the news of the Green Hand? I just had a battle with a number of the gang's men, and one of them bragged that he planned to dominate the entire country. I've been out of touch for nearly eighteen hours, and I'm worried."

Kirkpatrick's precise tones were weary. "You've every right to be worried," he said. "The Green Hand served notice last night that unless the Government paid five billion dollars, the gas would be turned loose on New York, San Francisco, Philadelphia, Washington, and several other of our larger cities. Tomorrow midnight—it's tonight now, I guess—is the deadline."

WENTWORTH FROWNED. "What's being done?" he demanded.

"Nothing that will do any good," Kirkpatrick told him. "People are rioting in the streets. Some want the money paid. Some want Jonathan Love made dictator. The town is lousy with those green-shirted soldiers of Jonathan Love. They've got a flock of fans set up, but I don't believe it will do a bit of good."

"And Love is in Washington?" Wentworth asked, his eyes narrow.

"Yes," said Kirkpatrick, "Love is in Washington. And the whole damn country is crazy about him. Newspapers call him the Savior of the country. They want him made Dictator, all-around-boss of the works."

Wentworth clipped out words. "That must stop. He's a tool of the Green Hand."

"Try and stop him," jeered Kirkpatrick. "I tell you the whole country is on its knees to him."

"It will take me seven hours to reach Washington," Wentworth said; "I'm going there and try to argue the Government into turning Love down cold. I don't expect much success. Will you assign fifty of your men to me and have them report to me in Washington individually at the Ambassador Hotel?"

There was silence over the wire. A gap of words which the singing of current in the wires filled. Finally Kirkpatrick spoke.

"It's damned irregular. They'd be without authority. Why do you want them?" he asked.

"I can't go into details," Wentworth said. "But Brownlee has a gas which will neutralize that of the Green Hand. The Green Hand will use fake gas chiefly against Jonathan Love. But he'll be using the real stuff too. I want your fifty men to use the neutralizing gas and protect the high government officials that the Green Hand will attempt to murder. He'll want to make sure his puppet, Love, is absolute boss."

"I'll do that," Kirkpatrick agreed at once. "Will you in return give me enough of that gas to protect the points of attack in New York City?"

"It's a deal," Wentworth said. "Remember, the Ambassador."

"By the way," Kirkpatrick broke in hurriedly, "those fingerprints you sent me?"

"Yes?" Wentworth was eager.

"They belong to a lad whose original name was Tim Selden. He did a year or two for robbery in 1923."

"Thanks, that's fine," said Wentworth, and hung up.

He had Ram Singh make further calls, one engaging an empty loft in Washington for Brownlee to work in, and others ordering the supplies he'd need to manufacture his neutralizing gas. Delivery was to be made by the time Wentworth reached Washington, which he estimated would be about noon.

As Ram Singh hung up, the plane which Wentworth had ordered was set down on a field near the station. Watched by a curious crowd, the four, Ram Singh, Professor Brownlee, and behind them, Wentworth with an arm about Nita, entered the plane. The motors roared instantly, the ship whirled, and took off for Washington in a mad race to save the nation from the domination of the Green Hand.

SEVEN HOURS, almost to the minute, after the take-off from Wacomchic, their big cabin plane landed on Hoover field. It was instantly surrounded by green-shirted troops. Wentworth still wore his disguise of the mechanic with the scar-twisted mouth. He let Professor Brownlee do the talking, and the Professor did it well, explaining that he was rushing to offer his assistance to government officials, seeking to counteract the gas of the Green Hand.

Finally they were permitted to enter the city and Wentworth, shifting his disguise to that of the blond and English Rupert Barton, in which character he was known to a number of the New York police, took up his quarters at the Ambassador and began making his arrangements for defense of the city.

Soon the New York police detail loaned him by Commissioner Kirkpatrick began drifting in by twos and threes, and Wentworth made assignments to each, based on maps which he had worked out on the plane. Each man was armed with a rifle and given a carboy of gas from Brownlee's loft factory down in the southeast section of the city.

Each man, with this equipment, was placed in a rented car and was given a specified section of the city to patrol. Every hour they were to phone the Ambassador for instructions.

"I don't know," Wentworth told each man, "how the gas will be carried, but I am making investigations and sometime between now and midnight, when the attack begins, I will give you your detailed information.

Wentworth's next task was to ship by plane a quantity of the neutralizing gas to Commissioner Kirkpatrick in New York. Then he gave instructions to Ram Singh, went to the Washington headquarters of the International Broadcasting System and had a long conference with the manager. His plans were complete now, except for locating the means by which the gas would be transported into town.

Bombs could not be dropped from the air this time. The city was too well guarded by circling planes. Wentworth knew, too, that the Green Hand did not intend to attack exclusively with the poisonous gas. He would loose large quantities of the non-noxious vapor for the worker troops of Jonathan Love to fight. He would free the real gas only at those places where he wished to wipe out prominent officials, who otherwise might prove an obstacle to the complete domination of the Nation—through Jonathan Love.

Wentworth equipped himself with a carboy of the neutralizing gas and a rifle and began to tour the city, seeking out some reservoirs for the gas the Green Hand had promised to release if the ransom of five billion were not paid by midnight.

He rolled along slowly through the traffic, following no set course except that now and again he intersected one of the patrols to make sure it was alert and ready.

Newspaper extra after extra was screamed on the streets. Wentworth bought them all. Love had been proclaimed dictator after a twenty-four hour cabinet session. He was given absolute authority, with the sole stipulation that he save the country from the Green Hand.

Still the panic was not stilled. People raced madly through the streets, seeking to escape from the city. Automobiles roared at top speed, loaded to the mudguards with humanity. All over the country, the newspapers revealed, this scene was being repeated. Panic ruled the land.

LOVE'S GREEN-CLAD troops were everywhere. The giant fans were stationed at strategic points, with reserve fans mounted on huge trucks ready to rush to any weak spot. And this, too, was true throughout the country. But it was here in Washington that the greatest forces had been mobilized. Love, himself was here, Dictator Love now.

Wentworth smiled dryly. He had hoped to forestall that, hoped to perfect his own plans and reveal them to the President in completed form, ready to take over the city's defense. Once

Love was installed in office, he had known, it would be twice as difficult to oust him. But Love was in office now, and still Wentworth's plans were not perfected. He had yet to learn how the Green Hand would transport his poisonous gases into the city.

A car ahead of him slammed on its brakes, stopping in three feet, and Wentworth squealed to a halt also. Another of those trucks that had been tangling traffic all evening lumbered out of a side street, rumbled through the snarl of cars it had created and trundled on. Wentworth rolled on, still pondering the problem of the gas. Another truck blundered into the street, tying up the swift, heavy line of fleeing cars. Wentworth stared at the bulky vehicle.

Like most of the others, it was a gasoline truck. The town seemed to be full of them, all heading into the city. As Wentworth, swerving to the curb with scraping fenders, hounded by squawking horns, a fleet of four more trucks, labeled "Shale Gasoline" droned past.

His eyes glinting, Wentworth began to hunt more tankers. On a side street, he found a fleet of four parked. And there was a curious thing about them. There were four men on each, instead of two, and Wentworth remembered abruptly that the others he had seen had been similarly overmanned.

Frowning, Wentworth sent his car swiftly back along Rhode Island Avenue, heading for the downtown district. It was growing late. In a little over an hour, the Green Hand's deadline would fall due. He would loose his fearful, murderous gases upon the city, seeking to wipe out all officialdom so that Love would hold undisputed sway.

Wentworth turned right after whisking through a large, double traffic circle, passed near the home of a sub-secretary of the Treasury. He saw a tank truck parked nearby.

Wentworth's eyes glittered. He circled a block so as to come up behind the truck, adjusted a small hose to the carboy of gas which he carried, and driving close to the truck, fired a rifle bullet into its tank.

Instantly, a thin streamer of green gas seeped from the hole. Wentworth spurted his car toward the tanker, thrust his hose out of the side and turned on Professor Brownlee's neutralizing gas.

There came a violent puff of flame, blazing instantly into an intolerable white heat!

Then Wentworth had swept past. The flame mounted higher and higher, until the trees beside the street began to wither with the heat. Four men piled from the front of the truck, guns blazing in their hands. Wentworth whirled a corner, heard a tire let go with a bang.

The auto lurched, swayed and, despite Wentworth's tight control, slammed sideways into a tree. Wentworth sprang out, gun in hand and crouched behind the car's motor. The four men pounded around the corner, pistols in hand. Wentworth's snap shot dropped one. The other three flung to the safety of a dark doorway.

The blazing white light of the burning gas threw eerie shadows on the street, made the doorway where the men hid black as night. Wentworth fired three swift shots into the darkness, then sprang from the cover of the car and raced to the wall in which the doorway was cut. Along this he crept toward the hideout of the three men. There were three guns against his one. If all fired at once, he would be surely killed and with him would die the country's last hope of escaping the horrible menace of the Green Hand.

BUT WENTWORTH'S course was not as reckless as it seemed. Only one man would be in a position to fire around that door jamb at a time, and Wentworth, with his uncanny accuracy, felt himself the equal of any one gunman. A pistol glinted, and once more Wentworth's weapon spoke. There came a cry of anguish, the pistol spun into the air and a dark figure reeled into view. Wentworth's second shot laid him dead upon the ground.

Wentworth called softly. "If I have to come after you, I'll kill. If you want to surrender, I'll let you live."

A shot blazed its answer. Wentworth's swift reply brought a curse of pain from the doorway.

"If you want to surrender," Wentworth called again, "toss your guns out where I can see them. Then come out with your hands high. I wouldn't advise you to try any tricks. Tricks always make me nervous. I'm apt to shoot first and ask questions later."

Moments of silence then, broken only by the distant moan of a police siren.

"When I count five," Wentworth said, "I'm going to start shooting. I'm afraid I can't wait for our friends the police."

"Gees, ain't you a cop?" a timorous voice called from the doorway.

"No," said Wentworth. "Throw out your gun."

A single weapon glinted in the air, clinked on the sidewalk and skittered into the gutter.

"Where's your friend?" Wentworth demanded.

"Cripes," the man in the doorway said, "You've killed them all!"

Wentworth's eyes narrowed. "Come out into the open with your hands high."

Promptly a small man with a pasty face stepped out. Wentworth's gun covered him, but his eyes were wary on the doorway. He saw what he sought—a glint of metal a foot above the ground. His pistol barked first, and the man in the doorway cried out in a strangled voice, and he spilled out into the open, kicking convulsively.

Wentworth had just time to affix Spider's seals to their foreheads and hustle his captive around a corner when a police squad car rolled up.

A taxi sped Wentworth to safety at the Ambassador.

He left the prisoner in charge of Ram Singh and told the faithful Hindu to order all the patrols as they called in to take every tank wagon they saw, fire a bullet through the storage vat and turn their gas on it.

They might make a few mistakes, but in that case there would be only the loss of gasoline to worry about. If the tankers carried the green gas, they would burst into flame on contact with

Professor Brownlee's neutralizer. He gave a few other final instructions in Hindu.

Wentworth's plans were now complete. He was prepared to expose Jonathan Love as the catspaw of a criminal—was at last ready to offer his services in the battle against the Green Hand. He went hurriedly to the street, found a taxi and climbed in.

"The White House," he ordered.

CHAPTER 18
DEATH TO THE SPIDER

THE TAXI driver stared curiously at Wentworth, shrugged and jerked his cab into motion. Whirling corners, he squealed eventually out into Pennsylvania Avenue and slid to a halt before the White House. Instantly a half dozen of the green-clad troopers of Jonathan Love were beside the cab. Wentworth paid off his driver and stepped out among them. A young chap, face fresh and rosy with the cold, stepped up to Wentworth. "No civilians allowed here," he said.

Wentworth smiled at him quietly. "Jonathan Love will see me," he said.

"Have you an appointment?" the young man's voice turned deferential.

"No," said Wentworth. "Just take him my name. Richard Wentworth."

The man stared at him dubiously, then jerked his head in a short nod. "Keep your eye on him," he told his three companions and strode off toward the White House.

It was fifteen minutes before he returned and bade Wentworth enter.

Wentworth strode between more guards at the gates, up the walk to the White House. On each side and behind him walked the green guards. He frowned as he approached the door. This was risky business, placing himself in the power of the fanatic, Love. But there was no escape from it. He must get his warning to the high officials, tell them of Professor Brownlee's experiment and seek to persuade them to seek safety elsewhere. Not that he expected to be able to persuade the President to flee.

More guards met him at the door, and at a word from one of those who had accompanied him from the gate, they made way. Wentworth strode into the broad formal hallway, was escorted into the Yellow Room. At one end of it, as on a throne, sat Jonathan Love, resplendent in the green uniform of his troops, a golden sash about his waist and a golden sword at his side. He was alone except for two stony-faced sentries who stood at his back, pistols in hand.

Wentworth stopped before the dictator.

Love did not rise. His gaunt, lined face seemed rigidly set, incapable of mobility. There was an exalted look upon him. Wentworth stood squarely in front of him, on straddled pugnacious legs.

"You'll learn, tonight," Wentworth said, "how futile your fans are. For tonight the Green Hand strikes not alone to build your prestige. He strikes also to kill."

Love leaned forward in his high-backed yellow satin chair, his left hand rested upon the pommel of his sword.

"Have a care, Wentworth," he said softly, "there are witnesses to what you say. Every word you utter damns you as an ally of the Green Hand."

"Tommyrot," snapped Wentworth. "Better accuse yourself. You're the one who's really helping that gang of crooks."

Love got slowly and magnificently to his feet. His uniform became his lean, long body. "Wentworth—"

"Oh, shut up," said Wentworth, "I didn't come to hear speeches. I didn't come here to see you. I sent my name to you, because you're the only man here who would recognize it and I must see the President."

"Well, well, look who wants to see the President!" a woman's mocking voice came from behind Wentworth. And the woman who called herself Olga Bantsoff and whom Wentworth called Maggie Foley, sauntered by, an insolent hand upon the hip of her green silk dress.

She turned and faced Wentworth tauntingly. Pale lips smiled; hate shone in her narrow green eyes. There was a sash of gold about her waist and she toyed with it. Slowly she turned her back upon Wentworth, strolled up to Love and put her hand on his arm. Once more she directed her narrow green gaze at Wentworth.

"When are you going to hang him, honey?" she asked Love. **HE PATTED** her hand. "You mustn't interfere in affairs of state, Olga. Run along, now; I'll see you later."

Wentworth stared at the man and woman, a sneering twist to his lips. "The Emperor of America!" he jeered. His voice grew strong. "Your empire is—Death!"

Wentworth turned and started from the room.

"Seize him," Love ordered.

The two guards leveled their pistols and sprang to intercept him. He waited until they were nearly upon him, then dropped to the floor and sent them in a sprawling heap. Before they could recover, he had darted from the room, along the hall and into the ante room of the President's office.

A secretary jerked up a startled head. Three Secret Service men sprang forward. Wentworth flashed past them into the office of the President. The Secret Service men were at his heels. They seized him as he confronted the warm gray man who was President of the United States. There were twelve other men in the room, government officials and members of the cabinet. They, too, sprang between Wentworth and the President, guarding him from the expected assassin's bullets.

Wentworth did not struggle against the Secret Service men. He was smiling quietly. And when he spoke, it was in a normal tone.

"Mr. President, may I speak a few words to you? It is about the Green Hand. I assure you that it is most important."

His words stilled the tumult in the room. The door slammed open and Love strode in, followed by his two guards. Love threw out his arm stiffly, pointing at Wentworth.

"Seize that man!" he ordered.

"Never mind, Love," said Wentworth. "I'm already seized."

"Just a minute, Mr. Dictator," the President interrupted. He turned to Wentworth, his grave, direct eyes studying him. "You seek your audiences somewhat precipitately, young man."

190

Wentworth acknowledged that with a bow and a slight smile. "Can you conceive of any other way in which I could have got here?" he asked.

"This man is a criminal," Love thundered.

Wentworth whirled toward him. "Will you shut up for two minutes?" he demanded.

Love glowered at him. His hand plucked restlessly at his sword, half bared it.

A thin smile twisted Wentworth's mouth. "Any time but now, Love, I'll be glad to oblige you. Foils, pistols, sabers, rapiers or poison gas."

He turned back to the President. "Mr. President, this man has been tricked. The country has been tricked into believing that he has a method of destroying the effects of the Green Hand's poison gas. I have positive proof that the fans are of utterly no use, that the gas used against him on the two occasions when the fans have appeared to divert it, was a nonpoisonous gas, released exclusively to make this man seem a Messiah.

"Tonight will tell another story. The fake gas will be released; but here and there about the city the real deadly article will be turned loose. Just enough to kill off every strong official in the country who might dare oppose the rule of Jonathan Love!"

"This is preposterous," Love broke in.

Wentworth ignored him. He saw that his own quiet demeanor was scoring a certain effect among the officials present. They bent heads together, murmured among themselves. The President's grave, tired eyes were unwavering upon him.

"I'm not accusing Love himself," Wentworth said. "He is only a catspaw, a tool of the real criminal."

"Who is the real criminal?" the President asked.

Wentworth shook his head slowly. "I still do not know certainly. A man named George Scott would be the only one I could accuse. And I know Scott is a false name, and that his entire identity is a disguise. I do accuse Olga Bantsoff. She has a criminal record in New York under the name of Maggie Foley. She is the agency through whom the Green Hand controls Jonathan Love."

A cry of rage tore from Jonathan Love. His saber rasped from its scabbard, and he struck an awkward, slashing blow at Wentworth. Wentworth threw up a hand in which he grasped his hat, caught the blade upon it. He seized Love's wrist and jerked the saber free, flung it to the floor. He put a hand against Love's chest and, with a thrust, sent him reeling back two paces.

"Nice little dictators don't lose their tempers," he chided.

THERE WAS a certain grim humor on the face of the President and the members of the cabinet. It was apparent to Wentworth that they had been forced by the people to accept this man as dictator and that they were chiefly amused by him. Still, there was the knowledge that two gas attacks had failed against this man's defense. And where he had not defended, thousands had died horribly.

"I think it would be wise, Mr. Dictator," the President said somberly, "to control yourself a little better. Undoubtedly what the man has said is irritating, but there is a time and a place for settlement." His voice was stern as he turned back to Wentworth. "You say you have positive proof. What is it?"

Wentworth looked him directly in the eye. "My unsupported word," he said. "And the laboratory experiments of Professor Ezra Brownlee."

"And these experiments?"

"Professor Brownlee," Wentworth explained, "analyzed the organs of men dead of the gas. He concocted a neutralizing gas which causes the poison to burst into flame. I have a patrol of men stationed about the city now with this neutralizing gas. Professor Brownlee says that fans would only increase the efficiency of this poison gas. He has found that its enormous ability to expand is based on its capacity for combination with the oxygen of the air. The fans, he says, bring in more oxygen and increase the amount of the gas.

A bearded man in uniform spoke up.

"Professor Brownlee was at Dunherst?"

Wentworth nodded.

"He was dismissed from there under suspicion of criminal practices?"

Wentworth nodded again. "That is true. But the charges were never proved. And I tell you he is as true and honorable a man—"

The uniformed man broke in again. "The charges were never proved because the chief witness against Brownlee was murdered. The murderer traced the design of a Spider on his forehead in his victim's own blood!"

What the man said was true, and that death had marked the birth of the Spider, scourge of the Underworld, gallant knight of Justice. Wentworth had killed a man who had framed evidence of theft against Brownlee, of whose reputation the man was envious, and whose wife he had loved. Yes, what the man said was true; but not a muscle of Wentworth's eyes wavered from their regard of the man. Not a muscle of his face changed, but he could feel a pulse throbbing in that thin white scar upon his temple and knew that it was red and angry.

"Those things are true," Wentworth conceded, "yet I cannot see that they affect, in any way what I have told you."

Jonathan Love strode forward, slapped his palm down upon the long table at the head of which the President sat. "I accuse this man of being the Spider," he said. "In Michigan there is a murder warrant out against him, charging that he killed five men, two of them with the gas that the Green Hand uses. He printed the blood-red seal of the Spider upon the forehead of each one."

The President's face had grown stern. "If he killed with this gas, then...."

Love did not let him finish. "It means," he thundered, slamming the desk again, "that this man is himself the Green Hand! These things that he tells you are intended to make you withdraw your precautions. Make me withdraw the fans which alone can defeat his poison gas.

"I tell you that it is all a treacherous trick to betray us into the enemy's hands! I demand that this man be executed at once as a traitor to the country that gave him birth!"

CHAPTER 19
VAPOR OF HELL

WENTWORTH SMILED at Love's out-thrust, accusing hand. The three Secret Service men clapped hands upon his shoulders. Love's two green-clad guards leveled guns. Wentworth raised his eyebrows at the leveled weapons, laughed.

"I seem to be considerable of a menace," he said.

"You are," shouted Love.

"However," said Wentworth, "if my legal memory serves me well, even a Dictator cannot order an execution without trial. Even if it's only a drumhead court-martial, you have to provide that.

"Mr. President," he turned and tried to bow but was held rigidly. He glanced amusedly at the clenched hands upon his shoulders. "Mr. President," he repeated, "I demand a trial and I raise objection to Mr. Dictator Love sitting as a member of that court. I am afraid he's slightly prejudiced."

The President's worn face was puzzled, his eyes intent and grave. "You are entitled to trial," he said. "As to the composition of the court, my powers are limited—"

"Surely the Commander in Chief of the Army—"

The President smiled faintly. His smile showed broad even teeth. His strong, cleft chin was raised. Above his high forehead the graying hair was slightly disordered. "Your trial," he said, "will be held tomorrow late. Then we shall see."

"Thank you," said Wentworth. Love was standing in rigid impatience, waiting for this moment.

"Take him away," he ordered. The hands on Wentworth's shoulder jerked him about and propelled him from the room.

He heard Love stalking, hard heeled, behind him. "My men will take care of him," Love said harshly. The Secret Service men dropped away. The two green clad workers closed in and with drawn guns ready, marched him out into the hall.

Love halted them there, a hard smile twisting his furrowed face. All humanity had gone from the man. He was in the full grip of his Messiah complex, fostered by the woman, Olga, encouraged by everyone about him. His lips were thin and cruel, his chin out-thrust.

"Take this dog out and shoot him," he said harshly.

His secretary, Crosswell, was coming out of the door, across the hall. At the sound of Love's voice, he turned, stared about in puzzlement, then saw Wentworth and the drawn guns. He strode close, his huge, incongruous body moving as lightly as ever.

"Pardon, Sire," he said to Love, "but do you think that such an action goes well with your famous magnanimity? You are known as a generous ruler. Would you wish to spoil that?"

The deep furrows of Love's face contracted. His eyes were burning with fanatical light.

"I am Jonathan the Just," he intoned, "but I will not permit the technicalities of law to prevent this man getting his just deserts. Take him away," he rasped again, "and execute him."

The men in green seized Wentworth by the shoulders and

thrust him toward the door. He threw back his head and laughed. "Jonathan the Just! By all that's holy, Jonathan the Just!"

One of the soldiers slashed at him with a gun barrel, and only Wentworth's quick dodge saved him from a nasty injury.

"Keep your mouth shut," the man growled.

"Certainly, Sire," Wentworth mocked.

They were out of doors now, bathed in the flood lights that were turned upon the White House from all sides. As they strode into the shadows, the man struck viciously again with the gun. Wentworth ducked aside and jolted upward with his fist, knocked the man sprawling. He dodged backward, and the snapped shot of the man on his left buried itself in the body of his companion.

Wentworth snatched the gun and struck again. The guard fell like a log. His companion, drilled through the head, lay motionless. All about the White House guards were shouting. Wentworth saw half a dozen of them converge on him—and then the gas sirens wailed!

THE FIRST one was far distant, off toward the northwest. Others picked it up, and their wails mounted to wild hysterical screaming. A police car shot down Pennsylvania Avenue, its siren shrieking wide open. A battery of fans to windward of the White House whirred into action. Their motors whined first, mounted the scale until they shrilled with speed.

Wentworth plunged into shrubbery, as the men who had raced toward him halted, transfixed at the sound of the sirens. They raced back to posts of duty, and Wentworth saw the door of the White House flung open, saw Jonathan Love, resplendent in gold and green, stride out into the night.

Wentworth crept off through the darkness toward the high picket fence that surrounded the grounds. Somewhere near here were two of his patrol cars, carrying rifles and carboys of gas. If he could get word to them....

Guards were pacing along the fence. Wentworth waited until one had passed, sprang to the fence and with a heave of his arms, vaulted clear. He fell in a heap and rolled as a blasting shot from the guard plowed the earth where he had fallen. Then he was up and racing away, zigzagging through the blackness. More bullets sang after him, but it was a song of disappointment. They missed.

Wentworth reached a pavement and slowed to a walk. This was where his autos were supposed to patrol. He paced along, waiting. No car passed. No car except a huge gasoline tank with four men upon its seat. Wentworth's body merged with the trunk of a tree, invisible in the shadow.

He knew what that truck meant, knew it was filled with the poison gas that struck down men instantaneously and killed them in horribly agony. Here then, was the source of the gas that was to kill the President and wipe out everyone in the White House.

All the truck had to do was to roll past the barrage of fans on Pennsylvania Avenue, loose its lethal vapor, and the wind would do the rest. The fans, sucking in more air, would help to generate the gas more rapidly. They'd send a great viscous cloud of the flesh-eater sweeping over the White House. Not a soul would escape.

Where were the patrols? Where were his men with their carboys of the gas that would turn this noxious vapor of the Green Hand into a pure white flame, harmless to kill and spread desolation? Wentworth drew his revolver, opened fire upon the four men in the truck seat. His lead flattened on bullet-proof glass. Guns blazed in answer, and the huge truck rolled on.

The tires were solid rubber; no good firing at them. Wentworth ducked from behind the tree as the truck rolled past, darted back into the parkland behind him, cutting toward Pennsylvania Avenue.

Even bombs would be of no avail against this truckload of death. They might stop it, but they would only loose the deadly gas, do it even more efficiently than the petcocks which would presently be opened. A parked car with the lights dark, caught Wentworth's attention. He darted toward it, plans forming in his mind for wrecking the truck by charging head on into it. He might prevent the gas from being loosed where the wind would sweep it over the White House....

He sprang to the running board. A man was slumped over the steering wheel, his head torn by a bullet. In the car beside him were a rifle and a carboy of gas. One of his own patrol, murdered!

Wentworth's face was a grim mask of hate. Gently he lifted the body of his patrolman from the car and laid him upon the grass. He sprang into the bloody seat, kicked the engine into life and spurted ahead. Already the truck had whirled into

Pennsylvania Avenue; already it was nearing that battery of fans!

Green-clad men rushed into the streets, aiming rifles at the bullet-proof glass that protected the driver and his three helpers. Even as Wentworth raced near, his cold engine stammering, green vapor, coiling, greasy fingers of it, rushed out of the hose nozzles at the tank wagon's back. They struck the ground, mushroomed and lifted thick heads like a nest of venomous snakes. They slithered, crawling, rolling, streaming, toward the fans, carrying death toward the White House.

Wentworth jerked the hose of the carboy into his hand, loosed the petcock, and with the neutralizing gas hissing from the nozzle, charged into the green vapors of death!

THE GREEN soldiers were reeling back, stretched in writhing agony upon the ground, the tearing teeth of the flesh-eating gas gnawing at their vitals. Wentworth's wheels churned the gas, as his own vapors spurted to meet it.

The world turned into white flame. Searing, leaping tongues of it raced across the earth, wherever the poison gas had run. The truck was enveloped in a blanket of fire. Wentworth felt its scorching breath, but he was traveling at terrific speed. Before the flames could do more than singe his face, he had burst through and was racing down a Pennsylvania Avenue that was lit as brilliantly as day by the leaping tongues of white fire that towered behind.

All over the city similar pillars of flame were stretching white fingers toward the night sky, as Wentworth's patrolling men pierced the tanks of gas, and set them blazing with Professor

Brownlee's invention. Here and there a patrolman was killed, and the horror gas got loose, drifting over the city, wiping out its hundreds before another patrolman could reach the scene and set it afire. Where the battle of the gases occurred, trees became charred stakes. Houses were enveloped in flame and destroyed in a few moments' time.

But in the end the victory went to Wentworth.

Everywhere people fled in panic, filling the streets with screaming, hoarsely terrified crowds. Women with children in their arms ran until exhaustion dropped them in their tracks. Grim-faced men, white with dread and anxiety, raced with them. But at last, when the tide of battle turned, they returned wearily to their homes, happily free of the Green Hand's death fog.

Wearily, at last, Wentworth too, left off the battle and returned to the hotel. This skirmish was won, but another, greater battle remained. The Green Hand was still at large, and Jonathan Love—Wentworth's face twisted with mockery—Jonathan the Just still was dictator.

His strength would be consolidated by the victory tonight. His would be the credit for the rout of the Green Hand. The country would be knocking its head on the floor at his feet, and the Green Hand would reap the loot of billions that Scott's scrawled figures upon a sheet of paper had revealed as its goal. Wentworth's smile was bitter. The Spider had not yet finished his task.

CHAPTER 20
JONATHAN THE JUST

B ACK AT the Ambassador, Wentworth conferred briefly with Ram Singh. "Did the *Missie Sahib* report?" he asked. Ram Singh bowed.

"And the radio company?"

"Han, Sahib."

Wentworth smiled. "It is well."

Ram Singh bowed again, left the room and Wentworth sank into a chair and closed his eyes.

Minutes later, stealthy feet crept upon him. The pasty-faced gunman Wentworth had captured was free! He stole into the room, his right hand gripping a revolver, and behind him, whispering encouragement, crept Ram Singh!

Swiftly the two strode toward Wentworth.

"Hands up!" the gunman barked. And Wentworth, jerking open his eyes, stared with apparent fright into the muzzle of a leveled gun.

He looked beyond the gunman to Ram Singh, and his face became distorted with anger. "You traitor!" he rasped. "False to your salt. Son of a pig!" He lapsed into Hindustani, his face still twisted with anger.

"Shut up," said the gunman. "You're making too much noise."

Wentworth cowered away from the man. "Don't shoot," he said.

The gunman grinned. "I won't if you're good. You're coming

along with me. A certain party I know will pay plenty to get hold of you."

Wentworth submitted to the man, and after the gunman had talked over the phone to four different parties, he allowed himself to be taken to the street, thrust into a taxi and trundled through the streets of Washington. Finally, at the side entrance of a great hall, the taxi drew up and Wentworth was hustled into the building.

"Mr. Crosswell," the gunman said, when a guard opened the door.

He was herded up dark stairs into a small cubby-hole of a room that was littered with stage properties. Ram Singh had disappeared somewhere on the trip upstairs, and the gunman crouched alone against a trunkful of clothing, the gun held carelessly in his hand.

A few moments later the door was thrust open and another man with arms tied behind him was hustled in by the green-clad guards of Jonathan Love. The man's face was haggard; deep lines etched into his face, and his wiry red hair was tousled. But there was a fight-gleam in his blue eyes. He glared about the room. His eyes lit on Wentworth, bound as was he himself.

His eyes widened. "So they got you, too, did they?"

Wentworth nodded slowly. "My own man betrayed me," he said.

Delaney smiled grimly. "From what I hear we won't have long to worry about it." He jerked his head toward the door. "Jonathan the Just," his words were a sneer, "is out there telling a crowd of fifteen or twenty thousand just how he did it. The street is full of them too and the whole damn country is tuned in on the radio. It's my guess that when he gets through, he'll haul us out on the stage and say, 'Here's the Green Hand,' and throw us to the mob."

Wentworth nodded gloomily. "That's a good guess, I suppose."

The green guards laughed. "A damn good guess," one jeered.

"All I hope," said Delaney, "is that they cut my hands loose first. If I could go out fighting, it wouldn't be so bad."

Wentworth grinned in spite of himself. That remark was so damned Irish.

A THUNDEROUS roaring filtered through to them, the crowd's shouting ovation to Jonathan Love.

"Sounds like we're getting near the end," Wentworth muttered. "Listen, here, Mr. Guard. I want to see Crosswell, Selden Crosswell, the big guy that's secretary to Jonathan Love. Get him in here, will you?"

"Aw, he won't come," said the guard.

Wentworth smiled dryly. "Tell him Wentworth wants to confess. He'll come fast enough."

The guard glowered at him. "So you want to confess, do you?"

"That's what I said."

"O.K.," the guard agreed, "I'll get him." And he went out.

Delaney looked at Wentworth with doubting eyes.

"What's the idea?" he asked. "Or are you really that guy, the Green Hand?"

"Who me?" said Wentworth. "I thought you were. How about the gang that shot their way into jail to rescue you?"

Delaney smiled bitterly. "They kept me prisoner from that day until this, stuffed away in some hole of a cellar."

"Think anybody will believe that?"

Delaney shook his head.

The door of the room flung open suddenly, and Jonathan Love stalked in. By his side, bundled to her ears in an ermine cloak, lolled Olga Bantsoff. Crosswell was with them, too.

"So you want to confess?" Love bit out at Wentworth. There was a fanatical exultation on his face. "That will be fine news to the crowd downstairs. I spoke first. They were impatient for me. But I promised my people that I would be back, that I would bring with me the Green Hand and that he would be executed on the stage where all could see!"

"And I," Olga thrust forward, hate gleaming in her green eyes, her pale mouth smiling, "am going to give the signal for them to hang you."

"How nice," said Wentworth.

"Well, get on with your confession," Love ordered.

Wentworth shook his head. "It would be useless," he said.

"What?" roared Love. "You got me up here by a trick!"

"I didn't send for you at all," Wentworth pointed out. "I sent for Crosswell. I wanted to talk to him. As I told you before, you have let this power bug go to your head. You think you are a great man. You're only the puppet of the master criminal calling himself the Green Hand. I know who the Green Hand is. When I am taken before the crowd downstairs, I shall reveal his identity and offer the proof. I think that even the crowd will be convinced."

Love snorted. "A lot of silly nonsense. I'm going back to my people. In ten minutes I shall send for you to be executed."

Wentworth smiled confidently. "It won't be I who is executed, Love. It will be another man, and that man will be the Green Hand. I tell you I have proof."

Love threw back his head and laughed. "Proof! A trainload of proof would not convince me that you aren't the Green Hand."

"I know that," said Wentworth, and mockingly cried, "Long live Jonathan the Just."

Love turned on his heel and stalked out of the door. "Come, Olga. Come Crosswell."

Olga followed with one last backward sneer at Wentworth above her ermine-clad shoulder.

Crosswell lingered behind. "With your permission, Sire, I will remain and see that these dogs are brought down for their execution at the proper time."

Love nodded carelessly on his way out. Crosswell took the gun from one of the guards.

"You men go outside and stand guard at the end of the hall," he ordered. "Let no one come near the door. I'm afraid that the gang may make some last-minute attempt to free their leader."

The gunman swaggered forward. "Listen, Chief," he said, "don't forget me. I'm the guy what brought him in here."

Crosswell smiled at him. "You won't be forgotten."

The gunman and the two guards went out. Crosswell closed and bolted the door behind them. Then, with the gun leveled, he advanced until he stood within six feet of where Wentworth was sprawled, bound hand and foot, upon the floor.

"I'm curious to hear, Mr. Spider," he said, "who it is you mean to accuse when you stand upon the scaffold."

"How curious are you, Crosswell?"

Crosswell leaned forward, thrusting out the gun. "Curious enough to put a bullet into your belly if you don't talk fast," he rasped.

Wentworth smiled pleasantly up at Crosswell. "The man I will accuse," he said, "is yourself, Selden Crosswell."

CROSSWELL STRAIGHTENED, smiling also. "I thought so," he said softly.

"You were damn clever," said Wentworth. "You almost made me think Delaney was guilty, just as you succeeded in convincing Love that Delaney and myself were tied up with the Green Hand. But I'm curious to know just what made you think that I was the trapper who killed some men in the north woods."

Crosswell threw back his head and laughed. "That was rather good," he said. "I see no harm in telling you, since you are so soon to die." He spun the gun around his finger by the trigger guard. "In fact, you're going to die before Love sends for you to go to the scaffold. But I don't think you could possibly convince anyone that I am the Green Hand even though I should be foolish enough to let you try. I've got Love too much under my thumb for that. Olga is doing a good job there; she has him completely fooled. And Love will do anything that Olga and I tell him to do."

He threw back his head and laughed. "Jonathan the Just!" he sneered. "Jonathan the Dumb!"

Wentworth nodded. "You're damn smart, all right. I showed how dumb I was when I tipped my hand by telling what I was going to say on the scaffold. But tell me, how did you trace me from the north woods?"

"It was very simple," said Crosswell "I had a spy in police headquarters. When you filed a complaint against George Scott, I knew you were the man."

"Then you were the one who phoned the guards at the Elkhorn plant and tried to have me killed, and you set the police on me afterward?" Wentworth went on. "You had Delaney accused of turning off that fan during the attack on Loveland, and later you had your men shoot him out of jail so that suspicion would be directed toward him—so that in the end you could hang him as the Green Hand and take Renee for yourself."

Crosswell started. "Oh, you knew about Renee, did you?"

Delaney surged against his bonds, tried to get to his feet. "You dog!" he cried. "So that's what behind all this! You want Renee!"

Crosswell nodded slowly. "I'll have Renee all right. But that's only a small part of it, part of the billions of dollars I'll get through Love's position as Dictator of the Government. I'll get government contracts and all sorts of concessions, not to mention a huge salary. Anything I want will be mine."

Gloating crept into his voice. "Billions!" he said. "Billions will be mine!"

He laughed around in triumph. Delaney raged curses at him,

and Crosswell leaned over and whipped him with the end of the pistol barrel, stretching the young Irishman unconscious and bleeding on the floor. There was ferocity in his face, as he straightened and glared at Wentworth.

"Some day I'm going to do that to Love. That fool, with his high and mighty airs! I was satisfied enough with my job, knowing I'd be rich some day, through him, but his airs got under my skin. I got to hate him, and now," he threw back his head and laughed, "he is the puppet, and I am the Master. When I pull the strings, he'll dance!"

HE CHECKED himself and glared down at Wentworth. "You're a smart man yourself, Spider. A pity we can't work together. How did you figure that I was the Green Hand?"

"By a number of things, Crosswell," Wentworth said slowly. "I'll admit that this Delaney trick fooled me for a long time. But I couldn't figure how Delaney planned to rule Love, once Love had become Dictator; and it was obvious that that was the crux of the entire plot. So I looked for a man of the build of George Scott, who could have a hold over Love; a man who could rule Maggie Foley; also for a man who had the opportunity to make the phone call to the Elkhorn plant and knowing your secret identification, give an order for my arrest. All these things, Crosswell, pointed to you.

"And then I did another thing. I got your finger prints, Crosswell; and they proved to be those of a notorious crook who went to prison at the same time that Maggie Foley, whom you call Olga Bantsoff, went up for highway robbery!"

Crosswell had grown restless during the recitation he had

asked for and which Wentworth had made more detailed than seemed necessary.

"Very neat, Spider," said Crosswell. "Now the time has come for you to die. Shall I shoot you, or Delaney, first?"

"Won't King Love be angry with you if you shoot his sacrifices to the mob?"

"I can take care of Love," snarled Crosswell and raised the gun.

Fists pounded on the door! A woman's voice cried out: "Selden, Selden, for God's sake, let me in!"

Crosswell whirled toward the door with a leveled gun.

"Who is it?" he demanded.

"Maggie," the woman's voice was hoarse. "Open up, Selden! The radio!"

Crosswell strode to the door, jerked it open. The door flung wide, and Olga rushed into the room, threw her arms around Crosswell's and pinned them to his sides. Jonathan Love strode in behind her, his face a thunder cloud of wrath.

"You dog!" he shouted. "You betrayed me. You are the Green Hand! We heard your confession over the radio."

"The radio!" Crosswell gasped. He was still struggling with Olga. Her blonde hair came down and streamed across her shoulders. "You will throw me over for that little tramp, Renee," she gasped. Her face was distorted with hate.

Wentworth laughed mockingly. "Yes, Crosswell, the radio. Every word you have said has gone out on a national hookup to millions of listeners throughout the country. I arranged in advance for this. Nita van Sloan made sure you'd come here.

My friends rigged up a microphone for this room as soon as they found in what prison you were putting me. They tapped in on the wires over which Jonathan Love was speaking. The whole Nation heard you confess.

"You're doomed, Mr. Green Hand, doomed!"

THE WORDS seemed to lend Crosswell new strength. He wrenched free of Olga, slammed her against Love, and the two sprawled to the floor. The woman clawed into the neck of her dress, yanked out a gun. Crosswell threw up his heavy pistol and fired point blank. The bullet ripped through Olga's forehead.

Love seemed stunned by the brutal violence of the attack. He stared at Crosswell, staggered to his feet, groping for the sword at his side. He caught the hilt, half dragging the blade clear.

"The puppet's master needs you no longer, Jonathan Love," Crosswell laughed, a little wildly. He drew up the gun and fired.

Love stared at him with wide, dazed eyes, then looked down at his breast, where blood was welling from his wound. He looked back at Crosswell again. His eyes rolled up and he pitched to the floor, dead, across the body of the woman who had betrayed him.

Crosswell sprang across their bodies, slammed and bolted the door. He whirled back to Wentworth.

"I'm doomed," he said "Thanks to you, Spider. But you're going with me."

Wentworth had struggled to a sitting position, his bound hands touching his shoes. As Crosswell threw up the gun, the Spider pressed a spot on the side of his shoe.

There came a muffled explosion, and Crosswell's head jerked back, showing a bullet wound beneath his chin. Wentworth had once more used the pistol hidden in the sole of his shoe.

Crosswell, swaying on his feet, trying vainly to drag up the heavy gun, had paid the penalty for the crimes of the Green Hand!

A crooked smile was on Wentworth's face. The score was settled. Delaney could be left here. He would go free. But the Spider, great as had been his service to humanity, still would be held accountable for the crimes he had committed for the sake of justice.

Wentworth's hands went swiftly to the kit beneath his arm, drew out a chisel, a duplicate of the one which had served him so well in the cabin in the north woods and began to hack at his bonds. As he worked, he spoke in the dulcet, singing tones of a Radio Announcer:

"This is the Spider speaking, ladies and gentlemen of the radio audience, the Spider, whom police hunt for murders, whom the Underworld wants to kill, because it fears his vengeful hand.

"I have just added another to my score of murders. I have killed Selden Crosswell, the Green Hand. You have heard his confession. Before I killed him, he had murdered the dictator, Jonathan Love and the woman through whom the Green Hand controlled Jonathan Love.

"The Spider pronounced judgment upon him, and the Spider killed him."

He severed the last of his ropes, slid the chisel back into his tool kit and slipped over his face a black mask, whose skirt dangled below his chin. Now only his eyes were visible, gray, and cold, with ironic laughter.

"This is the Spider signing off. Goodnight," he said.

He reached above his head to the dangling light, unscrewed the bulb and used it to short circuit the wiring system of the building. He stooped over Crosswell a moment, then in darkness crossed the room; in darkness threw open the door.

Moments later, police and a frenzied group of acclaiming men and women dashed up the stairs into the black hallway. Police dashed into the room. Their flashlights blazed. They found the bodies of Love and Olga Bantsoff, and Selden Crosswell—found on Crosswell's forehead, a blood-red, hairy-legged spot that was *the seal of the Spider!*

They found Delaney slowly regaining consciousness. Renee Love dropped to her knees beside him, took his battered head in her lap bent her lovely, generous mouth to his.

Police, searching the room, searching the theater, dug into every nook and cranny of the building. They found the hidden radio equipment and the secret microphone. But they did not find Richard Wentworth.

The Spider had vanished!

POPULAR PUBLICATIONS
HERO PULPS

LOOK FOR MORE SOON!

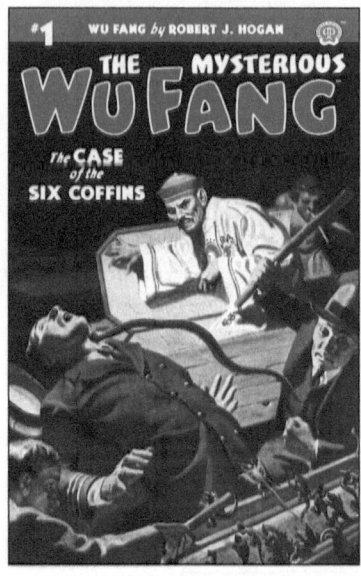

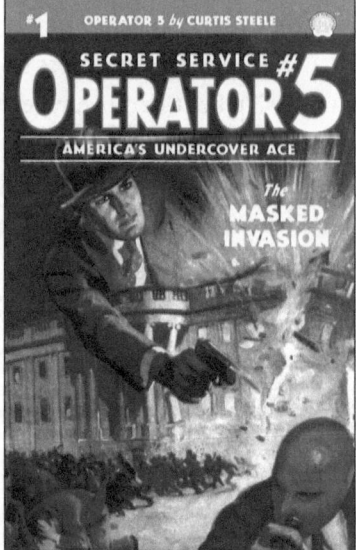